The Adventures of Caterpillar Jones

J.J. Brothers

Onjinjinkta Publishing

Onjinjinkta Publishing, a division of Gleska Enterprises.
P.O. Box 25490, Seattle, WA. 98125
1-800-433-8978

ISBN: 1-892714-03-5

Second trade paperback printing
August 2000.

10 9 8 7 6 5 4 3 2

Onjinjinkta is a registered trademark of
Onjinjinkta Enterprises

Printed in the U.S.A.

Visit J.J. Brothers online at:
www.caterpillarjones.com

Acknowledgments

There are a lot of people who are responsible for making this book possible, and we would like to take this opportunity to thank just a few of them.

First we would like to thank Dr. Melvin Morse, who taught us the importance of editing and rewriting. Instead of criticizing, he offered encouragement when we needed it the most.

Myra Moss, who told us how good our story was, and who made us believe in ourselves. She never gave up on us, and we really appreciate it.

Michelle Fryer and Georgia Carpenter for all the help and support they have given us so far, for pointing us in the right direction, and for getting us off to a great start.

Peter Orullian for not only correcting our less-than-perfect grammar, but also for giving us a lot of very helpful and valuable advice. Thank you for patiently answering all of our time consuming and often unnecessary questions.

Tom Eadie, who enjoyed our book so much he read it to his children twice. Tom never forgot about us, even when it seemed everyone else had. We owe him a great deal.

To our mother Karen for always supporting us, even though she would have preferred us to be doctors, lawyers, or even politicians. Anything but writers. Thank you mom!

We would also like to give a very special thanks to Betty J. Eadie, whose kindness and generosity has made this book a reality. She originally gave us the inspiration to write this story, and is now giving us the opportunity to share it with the rest of the world.

And most of all, we would like to thank God for making our dreams come true!

Contents

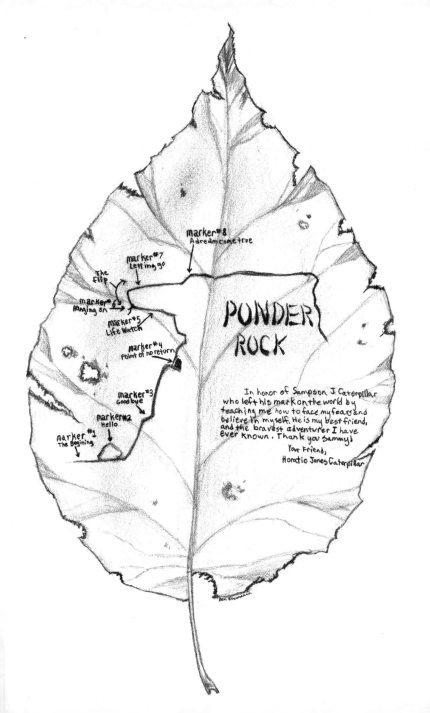

The Beginning

1

I awoke in darkness, trapped inside a cloth-like shell that cov-ered my entire body. I couldn't see or hear. I was alone. It was scary because I didn't know where I was or what was happening to me. I twisted and turned, trying to get out, but the cloth was so tight that I could barely breathe. Time was running out. I scratched and screamed, kicked and clawed, but nothing seemed to work. Then, without thinking, I threw my head back, opened my mouth, and bit down as hard as I could on the cloth surrounding me. I jerked my head back and forth, and finally the cloth ripped open. Morning sunlight came rushing into my eyes, and I quickly pushed my head through the opening and pulled myself out. I was free! Gasping for air, I realized what had just happened: the cloth shell was an egg sac, and I had just hatched as a furry green and yellow caterpillar. This was the first day of my life.

I let out a sigh of relief and said, "Wow, I made it."

Suddenly, something slammed into me and knocked me over. Before I knew it, I was on my back, staring up into the face of a young, furry, orange-and-white caterpillar. He smiled from ear to ear as he pinned me to the ground.

"Do you give up?" the caterpillar asked.

"Who are you?" I replied, confused.

"Oh, you are right. We haven't been properly introduced," he said, pulling me to my feet. "My name is Samson J. Caterpillar, but everyone just calls me Sammy." He shook my hand. "What's your name?"

I realized I didn't have a name yet. So, I blurted out the first thing that came to my mind.

"My name is . . . Horatio Jones Caterpillar," I said proudly.

Sammy looked at me and shriveled up his nose. "Horatio? No, that name is too hard to say. I think I'll use your middle name: Jones. Caterpillar Jones. Now that's a good name. But it's still a little too long. I'll call you C. J. for short. It's nice to meet you, C.J."

The Beginning

"It's nice to meet you, Sammy," I said to my new friend.

Sammy smiled and said, "Okay, good. Now that we've got that out of the way—"

Without warning, Sammy reached down and pulled my legs out from under me. As I fell on my back, Sammy jumped on top of me again.

"Well, do you give up, C.J.?"

"Uh, yeah, I guess so," I said.

Sammy looked disappointed. "C.J., you're not supposed to give up."

"I'm not?" I asked, confused again.

"No. Adventurers don't give up. Don't you want to be an Adventurer?"

"What's an Adventurer?" I asked.

Sammy looked surprised and quickly pulled me to my feet. "Do you mean you don't know what an Adventurer is? Ah, man. Well, I guess it's about time for you to learn. Here, sit down."

I sat on a small stone in the grass near a giant flower, and Sammy paced back and forth as he tapped his finger on his bottom lip, thinking about what he was going to say.

"C.J., being an Adventurer is the greatest thing you can be. An Adventurer always searches for fun things to do. He never gives up. And he lives the best life he can."

"Really?" I said, growing excited.

"Yeah, but it's much more than that." He picked up a small stick. "You see, when most caterpillars are afraid and run away, an Adventurer stays and fights." Sammy swung the stick around like a sword, pretending to fight the giant flower. "En garde," he said, slicing away a leaf. "C.J., an Adventurer isn't afraid of anything. And if something stands in his way, he doesn't walk around it like an ordinary caterpillar would." Sammy cracked the stick in half over his knee. "He climbs right over the top of it," he finished, puffing out his chest.

Sammy jumped onto the flower stem and began climbing his way to the top. The higher Sammy climbed, the more excited I became. Halfway up the flower, Sammy grabbed an old leaf and it snapped off. His feet slipped from the stem, and he dangled there by one arm.

"Be careful!" I shouted up at him and held my breath.

Sammy gritted his teeth and pulled himself back onto the stem. Without ever looking down, he continued his climb. When Sammy finally reached the top of the flower, he looked back at me and said, "You see, C.J., no matter what happens, you must always keep going. You can't let anything stop you."

A sudden gust of wind set the flower swaying back and forth. Sammy's eyes widened, and he tightened

The Beginning

his grip. "Whoa, whoa!" he screamed as the flower bent far to one side.

The weight of Sammy's body pulled the flower even lower toward the ground, until Sammy was hanging upside down right in front of me. We were staring face to face.

"Here, C.J., smell this flower," Sammy said.

I stood up and took a deep breath. The beautiful smell of the flower made me feel wonderful inside.

"Wow, Sammy, this smells great!"

Sammy winked at me and replied, "C.J., this is what being an Adventurer is all about."

"How do you know all of this?" I asked, amazed.

Sammy just smiled and said, "Because, C.J . . ." Suddenly, he released the flower, and as it sprang back up, Sammy did a full somersault in the air, landing on his feet right in front of me. ". . . I AM AN ADVENTURER!!"

My mouth dropped open, and I knew I wanted to be an Adventurer like my friend, Sammy. I wanted it more than anything else in the world.

Sammy taught me a lot that day. I learned that we lived in Mulberry Meadow. That at the edge of the meadow there was a giant mulberry bush that would be my new home. Sammy pointed out three dirt paths leading from the bush out into the meadow. The left path led to an old hollow stump, which the older caterpillars called Lover's Landing. The right path led to the home of E. Phil Snake—the most dangerous animal in the meadow because he was known for eating caterpillars. The center path led to a giant tree Sammy had never seen called the Tree of Life. All that day Sammy and I wandered through the meadow. And for many days that followed, too. Sammy never tired of teaching me how to be an Adventurer. And I never tired of learning.

2

Time passed quickly. I got older, and my body grew stronger. Sammy and I constantly searched for new adventures. We climbed the tallest flowers and explored the deepest wormholes. Sammy even tried to wrestle a mouse, once. Soon, our adventures made us famous in the meadow. But it was the event at RainDrop Run that made Sammy declare we had become legends.

RainDrop Run was the largest hill in the meadow. It stood just behind the mulberry bush. One day Sammy decided it was time for us to climb it. The climb was pretty hard, but when we finally reached the top, the view made it all worthwhile. We could see the entire mulberry bush from up there. It was so exciting that I could hardly catch my breath. As I stood

The Beginning

panting, I heard voices coming from down below. I looked and saw a group of caterpillars gathering at the foot of RainDrop Run. They were looking up at Sammy and me.

"Hey, Sammy, look!" I said, pointing down the hill. "I wonder what they want?"

Without a word, Sammy rolled a large stone toward the edge of the hill. He climbed up on top of it, stretched out his arms, and yelled down to the caterpillars below.

"My fellow caterpillars, listen to me," Sammy yelled. When he had their attention, he folded his arms, stuck out his chest, and said, "C.J. and I have conquered this hill in the name of Adventurers everywhere! From now on this hill will be known as Adventurer Hill!"

Sammy looked so serious, I started to giggle.

"If any of you dares to climb Adventurer Hill without our permission, you WILL be sorry!"

Trying to support my friend, I joined in. "Yeah, if any of you dares to climb Adventurer Hill without our permission, you WILL be sorry!"

One of the caterpillars began climbing toward us. "Hey! You boys better come down from there before you hurt yourself," he said.

"Uh-oh, Sammy," I said, "What are we going to do?"

"We have to defend Adventurer Hill, C.J."

"How are we going to do that?" I was beginning to feel worried.

"We are going to launch The Boulder of Doom."

Sammy jumped off the stone and began pushing it over the edge of the hill.

"But, Sammy, what if the Boulder of Doom squishes that old guy?"

"Don't worry, C.J. This is just a warning shot. He'll move."

Sammy pushed the boulder over the edge, and it began rolling down toward the old caterpillar. Half-way down, it picked up speed. The faster it rolled, the more excited Sammy got. "Yeah!" he yelled, as the old caterpillar dove out of the stone's way. The boulder rushed past the mulberry bush, down the center path, and out into the meadow.

The old caterpillar stood up, brushed himself off, and charged up the hill with an angry look on his face. "You boys have gone too far this time," he growled.

"Uh-oh, Sammy, I think we're in trouble. What do we do now?"

Sammy's eyes lit up. "We are going to have to use The Escape Pod!"

"What's The Escape Pod?" I asked.

Sammy looked around, desperately searching for something.

The Beginning

"*That's* The Escape Pod!" He pointed to an old brown seed pod on the ground.

Sammy ran over, tore it open, and began tossing the seeds aside.

"Come help me, C.J.! We don't have much time!"

Sammy and I threw out all the seeds and pushed the canoe-shaped pod to the edge of the hill. Then we sat down inside of it and shoved off over the edge. The pod zoomed down the hill, following the trail of the boulder. In seconds we passed the old caterpillar in a blur.

Sammy threw his hands into the air and yelled, "Yahoo! Look, Ma, no hands!"

I threw up my hands, too, and yelled, "Yahoo! Look, Ma, no—"

Suddenly, the seedpod hit a bump, and I went sailing into the air. I hit the ground hard and began rolling head over heels down the hill. The meadow spun round and round in my eyes, and I became dizzy. I felt sick to my stomach. I tried to stop myself by flattening out, but it didn't work. I was rolling too fast! At the bottom of the hill I grabbed a blade of grass, but it ripped right out of the ground as I rolled past. By the time I reached the mulberry bush, I was rolling so fast that everything was a blur.

"Help me!" I screamed, shooting past the crowd. "I'm out of control!"

I rolled down the center path, and it seemed I would never stop. Then WHAM! I slammed into something and bounced off. Lying flat on my back in pain, I looked up at the tallest tree I had ever seen. My head still spinning, I heard Sammy's voice off in the distance.

"C.J., where are you?"

"I'm over here, Sammy," I managed to say, still feeling sick.

Sammy found me and helped me to my feet.

"Is this the Tree of Life?" I asked, staring at the tree.

"Sure is, C.J."

"Why do they call it the Tree of Life?"

Sammy's eyes widened, and he became very serious. "Because this is where the creator of the meadow lives," he said.

"Who's the creator of the meadow?"

Sammy looked up into the tree, wonder showing on his face. I was a little scared because I had never seen Sammy act so strangely.

"The creator of the meadow is the Great Owl of Light," he whispered. "And what he does to caterpillars is so . . . ooooohhhhhhhhh." Sammy started shaking. "Just thinking about it makes me shiver."

"Why?" I asked, beginning to shiver myself. "What does he do to caterpillars?"

The Beginning

Still whispering, Sammy said, "When you get very old, and it is time for you to die, the owl comes to you in a dream."

My heart started to pound and my knees became wobbly.

"And in that dream," Sammy went on, "he commands you to climb up the Tree of Life."

"But, Sammy, I don't ever want to climb up the Tree of Life," I said, trembling.

Sammy grabbed my shoulders, looked me straight in the eyes and said, "You have to! All caterpillars must climb the tree! And when you do, the owl meets you at the top. Do you know what happens next, C.J.?" Sammy said with a strange smile on his face.

I was so scared that my lips were numb. All I could do was shake my head *no*.

Then Sammy pulled me closer and yelled, "HE EATS YOU!"

Fear raced through my entire body. I began to feel dizzy, and then everything grew dim. THUD! I fell down, out cold! The next thing I knew, I was lying flat on my back. Sammy was leaning over me, prying my eyelids open.

"C.J., you didn't faint, did you? Adventurers aren't supposed to faint."

"Uh . . . no," I said, trying to focus my eyes. "I'm just tired."

"Well, maybe you should go home and take a nap."

"Good idea. I think I will."

Just then, Sammy noticed a brown toad hopping by.

"See you later, C.J.," he said as he jumped on the toad's back.

When he got on the toad, it began hopping up and down. Sammy held on with one hand and put his other hand up in the air like a rodeo cowboy. "Yee Haaah! Giddy up toad!" he yelled.

As Sammy rode off into the distance, I felt like I had let him down. I knew I wasn't supposed to be afraid, but I was. I couldn't believe that I had fainted. I doubted whether I would ever be an Adventurer like my friend Sammy. I turned in shame and headed back to the mulberry bush.

3

When I arrived back at the bush, a voice said, "Son, if your head was hanging any lower, you would have dirt on your nose."

I looked up and saw two very old caterpillars lounging in the grass at the base of the mulberry bush. One was tall and thin and was sleeping. The other was short and fat and chewing on the stem of a leaf.

"Who are you?" I asked.

The Beginning

"My name is Clarence," said the short caterpillar in a slow, scratchy voice. "What is your name?"

"My name is Caterpillar Jones," I answered. "But my friends call me C.J."

The caterpillar smiled and said, "Well, C.J., you wouldn't happen to be one of those boys who were causing trouble over at RainDrop Run, would you?"

My eyes widened, and I quickly shook my head back and forth. "No, sir, that wasn't me and Sammy."

"Sammy? You know Sammy?" he asked.

"Yeah, he's my best friend," I answered.

Clarence nudged the sleeping caterpillar beside him. "Well, this is my best friend, George. Wake up, George! I want you to meet my new friend, C.J." Clarence began to chuckle. "He and Sammy were the ones who stirred things up over at RainDrop Run this afternoon."

My face turned beet red as Clarence winked at me. George only yawned, turned over, and fell back asleep. Clarence just laughed again.

"So why are you so sad, my young friend?" he asked.

I lowered my head again in shame. "I'm never going to be an Adventurer like Sammy," I mumbled.

"Why not?" he asked.

"Because I'm afraid of The Owl, and I don't ever want to climb the Tree of Life."

Clarence looked at me strangely and asked, "How come?"

"Because The Owl will eat me," I replied.

Clarence laughed hysterically. "Son, I think you are a little confused," he said. "If you really want to know the truth about the Great Owl of Light, then I know just the caterpillar you should talk to."

"Who?"

"The Reverend Kaleb D. Caterpillar, the oldest living caterpillar in the meadow," he said.

"Why should I to talk to him?"

"Because you need to face your fear, that's why. The Reverend was born back in late winter. He knows more about life than anyone I know. He's the wisest, most respected caterpillar there is. When he talks, caterpillars listen."

I looked around the empty meadow and asked, "Where does the Reverend live?"

Clarence pointed to an old bird's nest that was buried deep in the heart of the mulberry bush. "He lives up there in that old bird's nest."

I looked up and spotted the nest in some branches near the top of the bush. "How am I going to get up there?"

Suddenly, Clarence shot a thin thread of silk out of his mouth. It grabbed my head and reeled me until I was face to face with him. "Traveling Thread," Clarence said with a grin.

The Beginning

I was so amazed that all I could say was: "Wow."
Clarence laughed and bit through the thread, releasing
me. I wiped my face clean and asked, "But where do
I get Traveling Thread?

"You already have it," he replied.

"I do?"

"Yeah, here, I'll show you." Clarence stood up and
walked behind me. He put his hands on my shoulders
and pointed me towards the mulberry bush. Then, he
tilted my head upward.

"Okay, do you see that branch up there?" he said,
pointing toward a low hanging tree limb.

I nodded.

"On the count of three, I want you to take a deep
breath and spit as hard as you can. See if you can hit
that branch. All right, are you ready?"

I nodded again.

"Okay. One, two, three, spit!"

I took a deep breath and spit as hard as I could. I
was amazed when a line of Traveling Thread shot
quickly out of my mouth and wrapped around the
branch.

"There you go, kid!" Clarence cheered. "Now all
you have to do is chew your way up to the top. You'll
be there in no time."

I thanked Clarence for his help and began chewing
my way up to the distant bird's nest. I quickly became

very good at using Traveling Thread and couldn't wait to show Sammy what I had learned.

I reached the nest and pulled myself up over the edge. Inside, I found the Reverend deep in prayer. He was bent over with his hands clasped, whispering something about The Owl. I noticed his gray skin was cracked and wrinkled, and his tired legs could barely hold the weight of his aging body. I just stood there staring at him. On the way up I had a thousand questions I wanted to ask, but now I couldn't think of one. Then, suddenly, the twig I was standing on broke, and I crashed to the floor of the Reverend's nest. I laid there flat on my back, looking up at the smiling face of the Reverend Kaleb D. Caterpillar.

"Well, hello, Horatio. I was wondering when you were going to drop in on me."

I smiled weakly up at him and took a deep breath to gather my courage to speak. "Excuse me, sir, I was told I could ask you about The Great Owl of Light."

The Reverend nodded and said, "Why yes, what would you like to know about him?"

"Why do we have to climb the Tree of Life when it is time for us to die, so that The Owl can eat us?"

The Reverend looked puzzled, then upset. "Who told you that?" he asked sternly.

"My friend Sammy," I said.

The Beginning

The Reverend shook his head. "Oh my, Horatio, I'm afraid your friend Samson really has quite an imagination."

"You mean Sammy was wrong? The Great Owl doesn't eat us when we die?"

The Reverend slowly turned and, using an old wooden matchstick as a cane, hobbled across the nest, where he very carefully sat down on an old blue and white eggshell. Pausing thoughtfully, he said, "Young fella, like you, most caterpillars don't know the truth about what happens to them when they die."

I climbed to my feet, brushed myself off, and made my way towards him. "Well, what *does* happen to us when we die?" I asked, sitting down beside the Reverend.

He thought for a moment, smiled, and said, "Well, Horatio, when a caterpillar gets very old, and it is time for him to die, The Owl comes to visit him in a dream."

"That's just like Sammy said," I gasped.

"Well, not quite," the Reverend continued. "In the dream, The Owl tells the caterpillar that it is time for him to climb the Tree of Life."

"But not so the Owl can eat him?" I asked.

"Nooooo!" the Reverend answered. "The caterpillar climbs The Tree so that he may live in the sky with The Owl, forever."

"That doesn't sound so bad," I said, relieved.

"Actually, it's wonderful," the Reverend replied. "But before the caterpillar can climb The Tree, he must go through what is called The Life Watch."

A chill ran down my spine. "Wh . . . Wh . . . What's The Life Watch?" I asked, feeling uneasy again.

"When the caterpillar wakes up from his owl-dream," the Reverend explained, "he walks to the foot of the Tree of Life and begins staring at it."

"Why does he stare at The Tree?"

"Even though the caterpillar is staring at The Tree, Horatio, he is actually seeing something else."

"What?" I asked.

"He sees a long, dark tunnel with a bright light at the end of it."

I stood up in excitement and yelled, "What does he do then? Crawl down the tunnel?"

"No," the Reverend said, "the light begins beating like a heart, and as it does, it slowly pulls the cater-pillar down the tunnel towards it."

"Wow, that's sounds like a fun adventure for sure!" I yelled.

The Reverend shook his head and sighed. "Well, for some caterpillars it is fun, Horatio, but for others it is not."

"Why not?"

"Because as the light pulls you down the tunnel, memories of your life begin to appear on the walls of

The Beginning

the tunnel. Some of these memories are happy, but some of them are sad."

"I understand," I said, nodding.

"Good, because now we come to the light at the end of the tunnel," he said.

"What's in the light?! What's in the light?!" I was so excited I could barely breathe.

"An opportunity to climb into The Owl's world."

"Where is the Owl's world?" I asked. "Is it in the tree?"

The Reverend smiled at me. "No, it is in the sky," he answered.

"Oh, I bet The Owl's world is really beautiful."

"It *is* beautiful, Horatio, but before you can enter The Owl's world, you must prove that you are ready."

"How do I do that?" I asked.

"You must overcome your worst fear."

"How will I know what my worst fear is?"

"Well, when you go into the light, you will see a memory, a memory of something that scared you more than anything else. When you can relive that memory without being afraid, then, and only then, will you be allowed to climb the Tree of Life and enter The Owl's world."

"So when I enter his world, what will The Owl do to me?"

"I don't know. I have not yet met The Owl, but I can tell you one thing: he is *NOT* going to eat you!"

"But if you have never met The Owl, then how do you know he is not going to eat us?" I asked.

"Horatio," the Reverend said and gave me a gentle look, "do you know why he is called The Great Owl of Light?"

I shook my head *no*.

"The Great Owl of Light is the kindest, gentlest creature that has ever lived. He is very wise and very beautiful. His massive body is cloaked by a magnificent coat of pure white feathers. It is said that when the world was new, he ruled the skies. He is so beautiful that when the sun saw him, it became jealous and refused to shine while he flew. This is why he only flies at night. But even then, he still glows like a brilliant white light in the darkness. And that, my boy, is why he is called The Great Owl of Light."

"WOW!" I replied. "When can I climb the Tree of Life and meet The Owl?"

The Reverend slowly stood up and put his hand on the back of my head. "When it is your time, my boy. When it is your time." He nudged me toward the edge of the nest. "But for now, why don't you run along and have fun. You are much too young to be worrying about all of this."

A stern look crossed his face. "By the way. . . you tell your friend Samson that I need to speak with him.

The Beginning

His story telling days are over, if he can't keep the story straight."

I thanked the Reverend for talking with me. Then I climbed up out of the nest, attached a piece of Traveling Thread to a nearby branch, and slowly lowered myself to the ground. I was no longer afraid of The Owl, but I was still a little worried about the tunnel and facing my worst fear.

When I reached the ground, I decided to thank Clarence for telling me about the Reverend. I walked toward the base of the mulberry bush and found Sammy talking to Clarence and George, who was now awake.

"Hey, C.J.," Sammy said, "Come meet two friends of mine, Clarence and George. Besides me and you, they are the only other Adventurers left in the entire meadow."

I couldn't believe that the two old caterpillars were actually Adventurers. George eyed me, smiled, and continued the story he'd been telling.

"Like I was saying, Clarence and I call it Ponder Rock," George said, "because once you reach the top, it is a great place to sit and think."

"What is Ponder Rock?" I asked.

"I was just telling Sammy that it's a huge rock on the other side of the meadow past the Tree of Life. And that it turns ordinary caterpillars into Adventurers."

George looked at me very seriously. "You do know what an Adventurer is, don't you, C.J.?"

"Yeah, George," Sammy interrupted, "I told him a little bit about it, but I think he needs to hear The Adventurer Speech."

"Well, I don't know, Sammy," George began.

"Ah, come on, George," Sammy said, smiling.

George sighed and said, "Well, okay, I'll do it one more time. You see, C.J., being an Adventurer is, without a doubt, the very best thing a caterpillar can be. Now most caterpillars' lives are boring, but an Adventurer's life is full of pure excitement. He lives each day to its fullest, and he has a love for life that most caterpillars will never understand. He faces every challenge with confidence, honor, and courage. An Adventurer isn't afraid of *anything* and is willing to sacrifice *everything* for what he believes. He follows his heart, and no matter what happens, he never quits. He is proud of what he is, but he isn't afraid to change and become something better. His life is so wonderful that, even after he's gone, his legend lives on."

George finished, and I just stood with my mouth open. I wanted to be an Adventurer now more than ever.

Sammy turned to me. "Wasn't that great, C.J.? I never get tired of hearing that speech."

The Beginning

"It's not just a speech, Sammy," George broke in, "it's a way of life. If you follow these words, they will take you anywhere, even to the top of Ponder Rock."

"Tell us more about Ponder Rock." Sammy asked excitedly.

George laughed. "Oh, okay. There are two ways to get to the top of Ponder Rock: an easy way and a hard way. Now, anybody can take the easy way up, but only an Adventurer can climb up the hard way."

Growing excited again, Sammy quickly interrupted him. "I bet C.J. and I could climb up the hard way," Sammy boasted.

My eyes widened, and my mouth dropped open when Sammy said this.

Clarence responded, "I don't know, boys. In the entire history of The Meadow, only two caterpillars have ever made it up the hard way, and you're looking at them."

"You mean to tell me that you two are the only ones to climb up the hard way?" Sammy asked.

Clarence nodded. "That's right! Many tried, but no one ever made it until my friend George here invented The Flip."

Unable to control himself, Sammy jumped up onto his feet. "What's The Flip?" he asked excitedly.

"Well, you see, Sammy, most of the climb isn't too bad," George began to explain. "But when you get toward the top, there is a spot on the rock where you have to bend backwards and climb upside down."

I felt a lump in my throat as George described the climb.

"The climbing upside down part isn't tough, but then the rock curves back up again. That's when you have to do The Flip."

"How do you do The Flip?" Sammy blurted.

George folded his arms, leaned back, and shook his head back and forth. "No, I'm sorry, boys, but The Flip is top secret. I couldn't possibly tell you—"

Clarence interrupted. "Well, the first thing you have to do is find the root."

George frowned as Clarence explained how to do The Flip.

"The root is what you hold onto when you are climbing upside down," Clarence went on. "When you reach the end of the root, you hang onto it with your last pair of legs. Then you swing your body back and forth as hard as you can. When you think you are ready, you let go and throw your body upward toward the top of the rock."

My heart skipped a beat, and Sammy's face gleamed with excitement.

The Beginning

"Wow, that sounds great," Sammy screamed. "C'mon, C.J., let's go!" He grabbed my hand and began pulling me down the center path.

"Whoa, hold on there, boys!" Clarence yelled.

We stopped.

"The climb is extremely dangerous. George and I were much older than you two when we first climbed the rock. You boys better stick to the easy path for awhile."

"We will," I said with relief.

"Hey, wait a minute," Sammy said. "What happens after you do The Flip, George?"

"Well that, my friend, is the best part. Because after you do The Flip, you climb up to the very top edge of the rock. And when you pull yourself up over that edge, you will see the most beautiful sight you have ever seen in your entire life . . ."

"What? What do you see?" Sammy asked.

"The sun!"

"The sun?" Sammy said, disappointed.

"It's not meeting the sun that's exciting. It's being the first one in the entire meadow to see it. That's what makes it worth the climb," Clarence finished.

"Wow, did you hear that, C.J.? We are going to be the first ones to meet the sun tomorrow morning."

"Now, boys," Clarence interrupted, "remember what I told you."

"Oh, that's right," Sammy replied. "Uh . . . I didn't mean tomorrow morning . . . I meant when we are older. C'mon, C.J., let's go."

Once again, Sammy began pulling me down the center path. "Thanks guys!" Sammy yelled.

Clarence just smiled and said, "Be careful boys."

4

Sammy pulled me down the center path, and I asked him, "You're not taking us to Ponder Rock are you?"

"Of course I am," Sammy replied.

I stopped dead in my tracks. "Wait, Sammy, why are we going to the rock?" I asked, starting to feel fearful.

"To climb it, why else" Sammy said confidently.

Fear raced through my entire body. I began to feel dizzy, and then everything grew dim. THUD! I fell down, out cold! When I came to, Sammy was standing over the top of me, prying my eyelids open.

"C.J.," Sammy said, "I don't care how tired you are, this is no time to sleep."

I laid there a moment, looking up at Sammy. I shook my head a couple of times, focusing my eyes.

"But Clarence said we were not ready to climb Ponder Rock yet."

The Beginning

"C.J., Clarence doesn't realize that we are already Adventurers, and Adventurers can do anything."

"Oh, that's right. I . . . I forgot," I said as Sammy pulled me to my feet.

"Good, then let's go," Sammy said.

But my fear didn't go away. "You know, Sammy," I said, "I am still a little tired. I think I should get some more sleep before we climb Ponder Rock."

Sammy thought for a moment. "That's a good idea, C.J. You are going to need your strength." He patted my shoulders. "I'll go explore the rock while you go home and get some rest," he said and darted off.

I slowly made my way home, trying to forget about the climb I would have to make the next morning. When I got back to the mulberry bush, I snuggled underneath a leaf I used as a blanket. My stomach was all tied in knots, but slowly my body relaxed and I drifted off to sleep.

It was still dark when Sammy woke me up the next morning.

"C.J., wake up. It's time to climb the rock," Sammy said. "How can you sleep at a time like this?"

I wiped the sleep out of my eyes, yawned, and said, "But, Sammy, it's still dark outside."

"I know, C.J., but we have to get an early start if we want to make it to the top of Ponder Rock and be the first ones to meet the sun."

"You know, Sammy, I've been thinking . . . maybe we should climb the easy path first, just to get a feel for what the rock is like. Then we can climb the hard way when we get older."

Sammy just smiled and said, "That's a good idea, C.J., but I already climbed the easy path last night."

I felt fear building in the pit of my stomach as Sammy continued.

"The easy path is for old caterpillars and sissies, not for Adventurers like us," Sammy said. "It's not even as steep as Adventurer Hill. It's just a path that wraps around behind the rock and leads up to the top. It's nothing! That's why you and I are going to climb up the hard way."

I decided it was time to tell Sammy the truth about the way I felt. "Sammy," I said, "I don't want to climb Ponder Rock! Not now! Not ever!" Whew! I sighed with relief. "There, I said it. I'm glad I said it. I don't feel bad at all, I really—"

At that point, Sammy grabbed one of my legs and pulled me out of bed. As he drug me out of the mulberry bush, I looked up at him and said, "Okay, I guess you're right, Sammy. There's really no need for us to wait until we are older."

I felt scared as we made our way down the center path towards the Tree of Life, but I knew there was no way of talking Sammy out of it. Like it or not, I

The Beginning

was going to climb Ponder Rock that morning. We walked in silence for a while. Suddenly, Sammy stopped dead in his tracks.

"What is it, Sammy?" I asked.

"It's the Tree of Life," he said, staring straight ahead.

I turned to see what he was looking at, and then I saw it. The Tree of Life looked bigger now than it had ever looked before. We were so close. It was like a huge black bulk in the darkness before dawn. When I turned back, Sammy was staring at the tree with a worried look on his face.

"What's wrong, Sammy?" I asked.

"I can't help staring at it, C.J. Look! There is a tunnel with a bright light at the end of it! C.J. . . . I've started my Life Watch!"

My eyes widened, and I began shaking with fear. "Oh no, Sammy! What are we going to do?"

Sammy burst into laughter. "C.J., you will fall for anything. C'mon, let's go."

I paused for a moment and said, "Oh . . . that reminds me, Sammy, the Reverend Kaleb D. Caterpillar said that he needs to speak with you. He said your storytelling days are over."

Sammy stopped laughing and moaned, "Ahhhhhhh Man!" Then he lowered his head, kicked the ground, and slowly continued on.

It wasn't long before we found ourselves standing at the base of Ponder Rock.

"Wow, look how big it is, C.J.," Sammy said, staring up at the rock. "Isn't it great that we are actually going to climb it?"

I still didn't want to climb the rock, and I knew I had to think of something quickly if I were going to avoid it.

"Sammy, I don't think I can climb the rock today"

"Why not?" Sammy asked.

Trying desperately to think of an excuse, I said the first thing that came to mind.

"Uh . . . uh . . . my Traveling Thread isn't quite working right today."

"Oh, that's all right, C.J.," Sammy replied. "George said that *real* Adventurers don't need to use Traveling Thread."

I felt a lump in my throat. "I need to use Traveling Thread, Sammy."

"Why, C.J., are you scared?"

"Uh . . . well I don't . . . "

"Because if you are," Sammy interrupted, "then you can climb up the easy path like a sissy." Sammy pointed over to the easy path, which led up around the side of the rock.

"No, Sammy, I'm not scared," I said, trying not to tremble.

The Beginning

Sammy stepped up to the foot of the rock, stretched out his arms, and yelled, "Then let the adventure begin!" He turned back toward me and said, "C.J., we need to make some markers so that we can measure our progress as we climb. We might as well start right here. From now on, this spot will be known as marker number one, and we will call it THE BEGINNING." Then Sammy leapt up on a stone that was leaning against the base of Ponder Rock. He threw out his chest, held his head high, and stared directly at the wall of rock in front of him. "Hello, Ponder Rock, my name is Samson J. Caterpillar, and this is my friend Horatio Jones Caterpillar. We are Adventurers! So, prepare to be climbed!" Sammy looked down at the stone he was standing on. "This stone will be marker number two. We will call it HELLO." With that, Sammy reached down and pulled me up onto the stone beside him. "C.J., I'd like to introduce you to a friend of mine; its name is Ponder Rock."

I stared at the wall of rock in front of me and managed to mumble, "Hello."

Sammy smiled and said, "Okay, C.J., I'll race you to the top." Then he took a deep breath and started climbing.

He climbed very quickly and was about to climb out of sight when he stopped and yelled, "I will see you in the light, my friend." Then he continued climbing.

I took a deep breath, trying to bolster my courage. I didn't want Sammy to think I was a sissy. So I reached up, grabbed onto the rock, and followed after him. Sammy was pretty far ahead of me, but after awhile, I caught up with him. We climbed in the dim light of predawn that morning, one step at a time. Soon, I began to grow very tired. So, when Sammy crawled over a small ledge in the rock, I asked him if we could rest there awhile. The ledge was just barely wide enough for both of us, and part of my body hung over the edge. It seemed kind of dangerous and Sammy noticed that this was making me nervous. So, he traded places with me, which put him hanging over the edge. I knew then that Sammy would be my friend forever. As Sammy laid there staring down at the ground below, he began spitting tiny balls of Traveling Thread out of his mouth and watching them fall slowly to the ground.

"Wow, C.J., we are pretty high up. Before long, we won't be able to see the ground anymore."

Even though I was on the inside of the ledge, closer to the wall, I was still scared.

"I guess we better say goodbye to the ground," Sammy said. "Goodbye, ground, for C.J. and I will not see you again until we have met the sun."

Sammy paused and thought for a moment. "Hey, C.J., let's make this marker number three, and we will call it GOODBYE."

The Beginning

"Okay, Sammy," I mumbled.

"How far do you think it is to the top, C.J.?" Sammy asked.

"I don't know," I said. "But I hope it's not too much further."

Sammy just laughed and started climbing again. "C'mon, C.J., let's go. This is where we will say goodbye to the ground and begin our journey into the light."

I slowly leaned out over the edge, said "goodbye" to the ground, and reluctantly followed after him. I was still afraid, but by just focusing on one step after another, I fought my fear and slowly made progress up the rock. It seemed like we climbed forever. I climbed until I was sure I could go no further.

"Sammy, I am really starting to get tired. Can we rest again?" When nobody answered me, I looked up and realized Sammy was gone.

"Sammy, where are you?!" I yelled.

"I'm up here, C.J. I found a really neat cave." Sammy's head popped out of a cave in the side of the rock. "Hey, what's taking you so long?" he asked.

"I can't climb any further, Sammy. I'm too tired. I just want to go home."

Sammy looked at me. "Don't be ridiculous, C.J. Just climb up here. You can do it. You can do anything if you set your mind to it."

I shook my head. "No, I can't, Sammy, there is no way in the world I can possibly climb up there."

Sammy looked disappointed, but then his eyes lit up with an idea.

"All right, C.J., don't worry about it. If you can't do it, you can't do it. There is nothing to be ashamed . . ." Just then, Sammy's eyes grew wide and he looked scared. "Oh no, C.J., whatever you do, don't look back!"

I began to panic. "What is it Sammy?" I asked. "What's behind me?!"

"It's . . . it's E. Phil Snake, and he is going to eat you."

I began climbing as fast as I could, and before I knew it, I was pulling myself up into the cave beside Sammy. Sammy began laughing hysterically.

"You see, C.J., I told you, you could do it," he said, still laughing.

I laid face down on the floor of the cave, gasping for air.

"Well, we have wasted enough time here. Let's go, C.J. It's time to begin the hard part of the climb."

"The hard part!?!" I yelled, my heart sinking. "I should have just let the snake eat me."

"Oh don't be silly, C.J., there was no snake down there."

I became angry, and I glared at Sammy. "That's it! Let's go home! I've had enough!"

The Beginning

"We can't, C.J. We're passed the point of no return. If you would have told me that you wanted to go home sooner, we could have, but now it's too late. This is marker number four, and it's called THE POINT OF NO RETURN. We have to go on."

"Ahhh, man! Why didn't I say something sooner?" I said to myself.

"Sammy, can't you just go ahead without me?"

"No, C.J., we are Adventurers, and Adventurers must always stick together. Now c'mon, let's go."

I stood up and reluctantly followed Sammy out of the cave. We continued to climb until we reached the spot in the rock that forced us to bend our backs and climb upside down. Sammy went first. He climbed a little ways, stopped, and said, "C.J., I can see the Tree of Life from here. It looks kind of weird upside down." Then, all of the sudden, Sammy got real serious. "Uh-oh," he said in a worried voice.

"What's wrong, Sammy?" I asked.

"I think I've . . . I think I've started my Life Watch," he said and started laughing. "Sammy, how can you make jokes at a time like this?"

Sammy ignored me and said, "Hey. Why don't we make this the fifth marker, and we will call it THE LIFE WATCH. What do you think, C.J.?"

"I don't think that was funny," I said, still feeling a little upset.

After Sammy finished crawling through THE LIFE WATCH, he reached out and grabbed the end of a root that had grown right through Ponder Rock. He held on to it with his second pair of legs. He moved his body along and grabbed the root with his third pair. He kept moving and grabbing on to the root with one pair of legs after another until, finally, he was hanging on to the root with his last pair of legs.

I yelled, "It sure is lucky that the root was there, Sammy."

"It's not luck, C.J.," Sammy said. "It's marker number six. And since all you can do is hang on for dear life, we will call this marker HANGING ON."

After the sixth marker, Ponder Rock curved upward towards the top. Sammy tried to stretch his body from the root at HANGING ON to the top of the curve, but he couldn't reach it.

"Here it is, C.J.," Sammy whispered. "This is the spot Clarence said we will have to do The Flip."

My heart pounded as I watched Sammy dangle back and forth from the root.

"What happens if you don't make it?" I asked.

Sammy swung higher. "Then I will die an Adventurer's death," he answered.

"Don't talk like that, Sammy!" I yelled.

But Sammy wasn't listening. He just kept swinging back and forth, higher and higher. Then, all of the sudden, Sammy yelled, "Wish me luck. He swung up one last time and let go.

"Luck," I screamed as I closed my eyes and buried my head in my arms.

I hung there upside down in silence for what seemed like an eternity. Then I finally found the courage to open my eyes. Sammy was gone.

"Sammy, where are you?" I yelled.

He didn't answer. I held onto the root as tightly as I could, my heart pounding. I realized that I was alone. After awhile, I slowly climbed out to the root at HANGING ON. I just hung, dangling back and forth. I had no idea if Sammy had made it or not, but to find out I realized I would have to do The Flip.

"What if I don't make it?" I thought to myself. "But I have to make it. There's no other way down . . . or up!"

I took a deep breath and started swinging my body back and forth as Sammy had done. I gained speed, swinging farther and farther each time. When I felt like I was ready, I let go. My body flew through the air toward the top of the curve. I reached out and grabbed it with one arm. I slammed hard against the side of the rock, but I was just able to hang on. I took a moment to catch my breath and then tried to pull myself up. After a short struggle, I realized I could not do it with just my one arm. Dangling from the edge of the rock, tired and scared, I knew I couldn't hold on much longer. My hand began to ache as I looked down at the distant ground below. I tried to pull myself up again, but my hand slipped and I began to fall. Just then, Sammy grabbed my wrist and lifted me straight up safely to the top of the curve.

"Sammy! You're alive!" I screamed.

"So are you, C.J.!" Sammy smiled. "Congratulations, you made it. See, I told you we could do it. It's simple. The secret to doing The Flip is just knowing when to let go. In fact, let's make this curve marker number seven, and we will call it LETTING GO."

As Sammy named the marker, I caught my breath. I couldn't believe I was still alive.

"We actually climbed Ponder Rock, Sammy," I said, feeling proud.

"We haven't made it yet, C.J. The finish line is just a little ways up ahead. C'mon, I'll race you to the finish."

Sammy and I raced as fast as we could to the finish line, which was a small wall of rock. Sammy got to it first and jumped up and grabbed the top of the wall. He quickly pulled himself up. I followed after him. Sammy won the race.

When I got to the top, Sammy was sitting there staring at the sun.

The Beginning

"Look how beautiful the sun is from up here, C.J. And we are the first ones in the entire meadow to see it today."

I sat on the rock next to Sammy and felt the sunlight warm my face. The orange glow rose up over the horizon. "Wow, Sammy, it's beautiful."

"Just think, right now all the other caterpillars are living in darkness, but we are living in the light. Isn't it great being an Adventurer, C.J.?"

I nodded. "You're right, Sammy. This makes it all worthwhile. This is like a dream come true."

"This *IS* a dream come true," he echoed. "That is why we are going to make the finish line marker number eight, and we will call it A DREAM COME TRUE."

5

A whole week passed before we decided to climb Ponder Rock again. Sammy and I had both grown quite a bit, and I felt much stronger. The second race went pretty well, and I even managed to do The Flip without any help from Sammy. It was scary, but I actually did it. And as Sammy and I raced towards the finish line, I felt like I might beat him, but he was just too fast for me. Once again, Sammy crossed the finish line before I did. But this time, when I pulled myself up over the edge, I saw him sitting there with a strange look on his face.

"What's wrong, Sammy?' I asked.

Sammy turned to me and said, "C.J., I have just seen the face of The Great Owl of Light and lived to tell about it. At first I thought it was the sun, but when I looked closer, I saw the face of The Owl. I will never be the same again."

I knew from the look on Sammy's face that this was not one of his jokes—he truly believed that he had seen The Great Owl's face. I stared at Sammy in shock. Being first to cross the finish line, Sammy had seen the most powerful thing in the whole world. All *I* saw was the sun. I decided then that, no matter what, I had to win the next race. I knew I couldn't beat Sammy by outrunning him, so I would have to out-smart him.

We decided to climb again the next day, and when Sammy came to wake me up, I was already hiding in the bushes. As soon as I saw him coming down the path, I headed for Ponder Rock.

"Wake up, C.J.," I heard Sammy say behind me, as he burst into my room. "It's time for our third race."

Sammy must have waited several moments for me to come out, because I got a good head start on the race. But by the time I reached the base of the rock, Sammy had realized I had tricked him and was chasing me as fast as he could.

The Beginning

"Thanks for waking me up, Sammy," I yelled back, laughing.

I leapt up onto the stone, which was marker number two, said "hello" to the rock, and began climbing as fast as I could. I reached marker number three and looked down to see Sammy reach the base of the rock and begin to climb. I yelled, "Goodbye, ground . . . Goodbye, Sammy." I could see the anger on Sammy's face as he desperately tried to catch up. He wasn't mad that I had cheated; he was mad that he hadn't thought of it first.

"I will see you in the light, my friend," I yelled and began climbing again. But I was laughing so hard I could barely concentrate on climbing. The madder Sammy got, the harder I laughed. When I reached THE POINT OF NO RETURN, I stopped just long enough to tease him again. "Hey, Sammy, watch out for the snake. He just might eat a caterpillar climbing that slowly."

Sammy smiled and shook his head. He started climbing faster than ever, and I knew that if I stopped again, he would catch me. So, I climbed as fast as I could. I shot through THE LIFE WATCH and climbed past the root at HANGING ON so fast that I surprised myself. I quickly swung back and forth, did The Flip, and raced towards the finish line. When I was almost there, I looked back to see how close Sammy was to me. He was still too far behind.

"Sorry, Sammy, it's too late!" I yelled. "It looks like I am going to be the first one to meet the sun this morning."

I quickly pulled myself up over the finish line, and as I did, it was not the sun I saw, but a beautiful face surrounded by light.

"Are you The Great Owl of Light?" I asked.

"No, but you may worship me if you like," a voice said, giggling.

I pulled myself up over the edge a little more. It was then I realized that I was not seeing the face of the Great Owl, but the face of a female caterpillar. I stared at her for a moment in surprise.

"Oh, and by the way," she said playfully, "you were wrong, caterpillar. *I* was the first one to meet the sun this morning."

I felt my face turning red with embarrassment.

"Are you embarrassed because a girl met the sun before you did?" she asked, running her hand down my cheek.

This made me mad. I pulled myself up on top of the rock and stared at her face to face. "I'm not embarrassed," I said, becoming even more red. "And you were not the first one to meet the sun today, because you cheated, you came up the easy way! You have to climb up the hard way, like Sammy and I did!"

Sammy's head popped up over the edge.

The Beginning

She took one look at the two of us and said, "Who says I have to be as stupid as you two in order to be first? While you were busy climbing, I was meeting the sun." Then, she looked at me straight in the eyes and said, "So, I win, and you lose!"

I turned to Sammy for support, but he was trying to hide underneath the edge of the finish line. She saw him and laughed even harder, which made me even madder. How could she cheat by not climbing the hard way and say she won. I was about to tell her how I felt, when she did something terrible, something too horrifying to even imagine. She kissed me! Fear raced through my entire body. I began to feel dizzy, and then everything grew dim. THUD! I fell down, out cold! Again!

Hello

When I came to, I realized my life would never be the same, for I was looking into the eyes of the most beauti-ful creature I had ever seen. As I tried to stand up, she guided me back down and took my hand.

"Are you okay.?" she asked. "I didn't mean to scare you."

"I'm not scared," I yelled as I pushed her hand away and jumped back up onto my feet. "Sammy and I are never scared. Isn't that right, Sammy?"

Sammy's head slowly peaked up over the edge of the finish line. "That's right," he yelled and quickly ducked back out of sight.

Hello

"Who was that?" she asked curiously.

"That's my friend, Sammy," I said.

"Oh . . . what's your name?"

I threw my head back and stuck out my chest. "My name is Horatio Jones Caterpillar," I said proudly in my deepest voice. "But you can call me C.J."

"C.J.?" She smiled and thought for a moment. "No . . . I think I'll just call you Jones." She reached out and shook my hand. "Hello, Jones, it's nice to meet you. My name is Joan B. Caterpillar, but you can call me Cat. I'm sorry if I ruined your race."

"Oh that's all right, Cat," I quickly answered. "Sammy and I race all the time. It's no big deal."

Cat turned around and began to walk away, speaking over her shoulder. "Well it was nice to meet you, Jones. Maybe I will see you around some time."

"Uh . . . wait, Cat, don't leave." For some reason, I didn't want her to leave, at least not without me.

She stopped and turned around.

"Uh . . . what I mean is . . . uh . . . walking down the path could be kind of dangerous for a girl. Uh . . . maybe I should go with you. You know, just to make sure you get down safely."

Cat smiled at me. "Maybe you're right, Jones. That path is kind of dangerous. It would be nice to have a big strong caterpillar like you to help me down."

I confidently smiled as I took her hand and guided her down the easy path.

"Hey, what about your friend?" Cat stopped and looked back.

"Oh, yeah," I said, looking back toward the finish line.

"Hey, Sammy, do you want to come with us?"

"No thanks," Sammy yelled, still hiding.

"Okay, well, I'll see you later." I took Cat's hand once again, and we continued down the easy path.

I spent the rest of the day talking with Cat, and by the time the sun had set, we were friends.

As the days went by, Sammy and I climbed Ponder Rock several more times. Sometimes I would win and sometimes Sammy would win. Cat met me after every race, which made me feel like a winner, even when I lost. And each time, we would hold hands as we walked back to the mulberry bush.

Cat and I began spending a lot of time together. We talked for hours about everything we could think of. She was born in early spring, which meant she was quite a bit older than me. But this didn't make much difference, because it always felt like we were the same age. I thought that Cat was the most beautiful creature I had ever seen. I loved to look at her big yellow eyes, which reflected the sun, and her gentle lips, which caught the rain. Her body was as green as the grass, and her yellow spots dotted it like dandelions. She was as beautiful as she was fun, and each night I fell asleep thinking about her.

Hello

One morning, she woke me up with a kiss.

"Wake up, Jones," she said. "We're going to be late."

"Where are we going, Cat?" I asked.

"You'll see," she said as she grabbed my hand and led me out of the mulberry bush.

We were half way down the left path, when I realized she was leading me to the hollow stump that the older caterpillars called Lover's Landing.

"Cat, I don't want to go to that boring old stump," I grumbled.

Cat stopped quickly and looked at me.

"Lover's Landing is not boring, Jones," she said angrily. "It's beautiful. Come, you'll see."

"Oh, all right," I groaned and let her continue to pull me down the path.

I loved being with Cat, but moments like this made me miss being with Sammy. When we finally reached the stump, Cat's eyes lit up with excitement.

"See, Jones, I told you it was beautiful."

"Yeah, you're right, Cat, it is beautiful. Can we go home now?" I said, starting back toward the mulberry bush.

"No, we can't go home, Jones! We haven't climbed it yet!"

I stopped abruptly and whirled around. "Oh yeah, now you're talkin'!" Now I saw that old, hollow stump in a whole new light. "Okay, Cat, you go first," I said.

Cat walked to the base of the stump. "All right, here I go," she said and spit a line of Traveling Thread to the top.

"What are you doing?" I asked. "You're not supposed to use Traveling Thread. It's against the rules."

"But, Jones, I have never climbed without using Traveling Thread. I'm not sure I can do it."

"Sure you can, Cat, it is easy. Here, I'll teach you." I began climbing up the stump. "All you have to do is keep a steady grip with both hands, and then slowly pull your way up."

I reached down and grabbed Cat's arm. She quickly pulled away.

"No, Jones, I have to do this on my own."

"Oh, okay," I said. "You keep going. I'll climb up ahead and wait for you at the top."

I continued climbing. Just as I was about to reach the top, I noticed a tunnel in the stump. It was dark, and I couldn't see very far inside. I wondered how long the tunnel was. I knew I had plenty of time before Cat would reach me, so I decided to climb in and do some exploring. I was only half way in, when the tunnel got too narrow for me to crawl in any further. As I tried to climb back out of the tunnel, I couldn't move. I was stuck! My head was buried deep inside the stump, and I was running out of air. I rocked my body back and forth, but my head would not budge.

Hello

"Help! Help!" I screamed, and I began to panic.

I pushed as hard as I could, but no matter how hard I tried, I couldn't move. I was just about to run out of air, when Cat grabbed my back legs and pulled me out of the darkness. I felt weak, and I took a huge gasp of air and tried to focus my eyes. It was then that I realized I was being carried to the top of the stump. When we reached the top, I fell flat on my back, still gasping for air. My eyes finally focused, and I looked up to find Cat staring down at me. She was shaking her head back and forth.

"I know you want to be an Adventurer, Jones, but you have got to be more careful."

"Oh thank you for saving me, Cat," I said, still panting. "I don't know where I would be without you."

Cat just sighed and said, "You'd still be stuck in that hole."

I began to laugh as Cat pulled me back up onto my feet. I held her hand, and we stared out into the meadow. From the top of the stump we could see the Tree of Life and the mulberry bush without even turning our heads. It was truly an amazing sight, one I knew I would want to return to.

Cat and I spent the entire day up on Lover's Landing. Before I knew it, the sun was beginning to set. As it slowly disappeared behind Adventurer Hill, Cat and I stared out into the orange glow that lit up the horizon. I felt a feeling I had never felt before; it was warm and peaceful. We sat there in silence for awhile. Then, suddenly, Cat turned to me.

"Isn't it beautiful, Jones?" she asked.

"Well I really—"

Before I could finish what I was saying, Cat took me into her arms, stared deep into my eyes, and kissed me. As she pulled away, she whispered, "I love you, Jones."

I stared into her eyes and whispered back, "I love you too, Cat. You're right, this place *IS* beautiful. And you're beautiful, too."

After that day, Cat and I spent a lot of time on top of Lover's Landing. We shared our dreams and told each other our deepest secrets. But as time went on, I began to feel sorry for Sammy. He didn't have anyone he could share his dreams with, or tell his secrets to. He just spent a lot of time alone, climbing Ponder Rock and getting himself into trouble. He said he didn't mind being alone, but I know he did. He was lonely, and I knew it.

Then one day I got an idea. Cat had a girlfriend named Sandy, and she was alone, too. So, Cat and I decided to introduce them to each other. They agreed to meet and were both very excited when the day came. Sammy was nervous when he met me at the base of the mulberry bush that morning. He never combed his hair, but that day his hair was parted down the middle and combed to the sides. He was even wearing a bow tie made out of Traveling Thread.

"How do I look, C.J.?" Sammy asked anxiously. "Do I look all right?"

"You look fine," I replied as we walked out into the meadow.

"What if she doesn't like me?" Sammy asked, leaning over to pick a small flower from the ground. "Do you really think she will like me?"

I stopped and looked at him. "Sammy, are you scared?" I asked. "Adventurers aren't supposed to be—"

"Heck no, I'm not scared," he exclaimed and threw down the flower and stomped on it. "Huh . . . scared . . . I'm sure I'm going to be afraid of a stupid girl."

Sammy continued mumbling as he marched out into the meadow. I just laughed and followed after him. We were going to meet Cat and Sandy out in the middle of the meadow. We had decided to have a picnic. Cat would bring a large leaf for us to sit on, and Sandy would bring several small leaves for us to eat. When we finally got there, Sammy and Sandy were both a little nervous, but the two of them hit it off immediately. All through dinner, Sammy told jokes, and Sandy laughed at every one of them. She even laughed at the ones that weren't funny. The picnic ended, and Sammy asked Sandy if she wanted to go for a walk. She said yes, and they joined hands and walked out into the meadow.

Seeing Sammy and Sandy together made me realize that I wanted to spend the rest of my life with Cat. So, the next day, I told Cat to meet me at the top of Lover's Landing. It was there that I was going to ask her to marry me.

When Cat finally arrived, I wasted no time in asking the most important question of our lives. "Cat, will you make me the happiest caterpillar in the meadow and become my wife?"

Cat gave me a look that I had never seen before. "Oh Jones," she said, "I'm so happy, I could . . . "

Suddenly, Cat stopped talking. She tried to speak, but she couldn't. Her forehead tightened, and her eyes filled with water. After awhile, the water began to overflow and spill down her cheeks. This worried me.

"What's wrong?" I asked.

"Nothing is wrong, Jones," Cat replied. "I'm just so happy that my heart is letting the sorrow leave me. Don't you know about crying?"

"No, Cat, Sammy never taught me about crying. I guess Adventurers aren't supposed to cry."

"That is ridiculous, Jones, everybody cries."

"What is crying, Cat?"

Hello

Cat thought for a moment and said, "Well, Jones, sometimes, when you are really sad or really happy, your heart begins to fill with tears. When your heart is full, the tears begin to overflow. They climb up out of your heart and flow out of your eyes. Then they roll down your face and onto the ground, taking the sadness with them."

"Well . . . I don't like to see you cry, Cat. It makes me feel bad."

"No, Jones, you don't understand. Sometimes tears can be beautiful."

I was a little confused. "But I don't understand. Why do we have to cry?" I asked.

"Because, Jones, if you don't, then the tears will fill up your heart, and you will carry that sadness around inside of you forever." She gave me a serious look.

"Wow, Cat!" I said. "That sounds pretty important. How do you do it?" I asked.

Cat just smiled and said, "It's not something you do, it's something that happens to you."

"Well why did it happen to you? Are you sad, Cat?" I asked confused.

"Oh no, Jones, I am not sad. I'm happy. I'm happier than I have ever been in my entire life."

After hearing these words, I stared deep into her eyes and asked, "Does this mean you will marry me?"

Cat's face lit up, and she fell back into my arms.

"Oh yes, Jones. I will! I will marry you!" she shouted.

I was so happy that I almost dropped her.

The day of our marriage was beautiful. The early morning sun broke through the clouds and warmed the surface of Ponder Rock, which was where the wedding was to take place. Sammy was my best man, of course, and Sandy was Cat's maid of honor. We all stood on the mighty rock and looked out over the beautiful flowers that colored the floor of the meadow. When the ceremony began, the Reverend Kaleb D. Caterpillar stood in the center of Ponder Rock, his back to the finish line, and faced us. We were all very nervous . . . until the Reverend spoke.

"Will the best man and the maid of honor please check to see if the drop area is safe."

"That's us," Sammy said to Sandy. They joined hands and made their way to the top of the curve at LETTING GO.

As they checked the drop area, I found myself staring at Cat. She looked more beautiful to me than ever before. A veil of Traveling Thread covered her face, but her eyes still sparkled underneath. Cat noticed that I was staring at her, and she winked at me.

"Boy, it sure is a long way down," Sandy said nervously, looking down over the edge.

Hello

Just then, a piece of the rock that Sandy was standing on broke loose, and she began to fall. Without even thinking, Sammy quickly reached over and pulled her to safety. But as he raised her to her feet, he lost his balance. Sammy slipped off the edge of the rock and fell towards the ground. Sandy tucked her face into her hands and started screaming. Cat and the Reverend raced over to see if they could help, but it was too late. Sammy was gone.

Cat turned towards me and screamed, "Jones, what are we going to do? Sammy fell off the rock."

"I'll tell you what we are going to do," I replied as I slowly walked over to the edge. "First we are going to get Sammy to stop fooling around, and then we are going to finish getting married."

I reached the edge and looked down to find Sammy hanging upside down from the root at HANGING ON. He had his arms folded over his chest. He was swinging back and forth, and he had a big smile on his face.

He looked up and asked, "C.J., do you think if the world was upside-down, bats would sleep standing up?"

"Sammy, do you think that it would be possible for you to quit messing around long enough for me to get married?"

Sammy flipped himself up onto the top of the curve, like he had done so many times before in our early morning races. Then he brushed himself off, shrugged his shoulders, and said, "Sure, what are we waiting for?" He turned to the Reverend and said, "The drop area looks good to me."

Cat and Sandy started to giggle, but the Reverend didn't find him funny at all. He glared at Sammy with a stern look on his face and said, "Samson, I would like to have a word with you after the ceremony."

Sammy stopped laughing, stood there a moment, and said, "Ahhhhhh, man." Then he lowered his head and kicked the ground.

Sandy walked over and whispered to him, "Thank you for saving my life, Sammy. You're my hero." She winked at him and followed Cat and the Reverend as they walked away. Sammy looked over at me with a devilish grin on his face and nodded his head confidently. I just smiled, put my arm around Sammy, and walked back to the ceremony.

The rest of the wedding went perfectly. The Reverend talked about The Owl and how he would protect us all. Then he turned to me and said, "Horatio, do you take Joan to be your wedded wife. To have and to hold, from this day forward, until death do you part?"

"I do," I said.

Then the Reverend asked Cat the same question. When she said "I do," I was happier than I had ever been before. Cat and I joined hands and walked out to the edge of the curve.

The Reverend continued to speak, "The Owl will watch over you and protect you. And as long as you believe in him and in each other, your love will last forever."

I looked at Cat. She smiled and winked at me. Then she softly whispered the word "forever." A warm feeling filled my heart, and I knew we would be together for eternity.

The Reverend told us to attach a piece of Traveling Thread to the top of the curve. We attached our threads, and the Reverend spoke once more. "Marriage is like a leap of faith, and you must trust that your love will bring you together. You may now kiss the bride."

When the Reverend finished, Cat and I jumped off the edge and began slowly falling toward the ground. My Traveling Thread wrapped around hers as Cat and I began spinning around each other in a circle. The farther we fell, the smaller the circle became, our threads twisting more tightly together. By the time we reached the bottom, the threads had pulled us close to one another, and our mouths were touching. As we landed on the ground, holding each other, I was kissing my bride.

Goodbye

After we were married, Cat and I spent almost all of our time together. It didn't matter where we went, or what we did; just being together was enough. She knew how to cheer me up when I was sad, and she made me laugh almost as much as Sammy did.

Sammy finally built up enough courage to ask Sandy to marry him. They were married on the top of Ponder Rock, just like Cat and I. Their ceremony was almost the same as ours, except that Sammy and I began the ceremony by climbing Ponder Rock the hard way. When we finished the race, Sandy, Cat, and the Reverend met us at the top. I had never seen Sammy

Goodbye

more happy than on that day, not even when we went on adventures.

Time passed quickly, and soon it was midsummer. Sammy and I were older now, and since we were both married, it was hard to spend much time together. We talked once in awhile, but I spent most of my time with Cat. Cat and I climbed Lover's Landing several times, usually at dusk. We loved watching the sunset together, and each sunset seemed more beautiful than the last one.

As the days went by, I began to notice that Cat was growing older. Her skin was getting wrinkled, and she didn't have as much energy as she used to. Still, I thought she was growing more beautiful with age. The fact that she was growing older never seemed to bother Cat, until one chilly summer morning. It was a morning which changed our lives forever.

Sammy woke Cat and I with the news that the Reverend Kaleb D. Caterpillar had just started his Life Watch and was about to climb the Tree of Life. When we got to the foot of the tree, there was a large group of caterpillars gathered around it, and the Reverend was about to speak.

"I'm sorry, my friends," the Reverend said as he raised his hands up in the air, quieting the crowd. "But I am afraid it is time for me to leave the meadow. You see, The Great Owl of Light visited me in a dream last night and told me it was time for me to climb the Tree of Life."

Suddenly, Cat's sadness overtook her, and she raced towards the Reverend's side. I quickly followed after her.

"Reverend, wait, you can't go!" she screamed. Tears filled her eyes. "If you leave, who will take care of us?"

"You can take care of each other," the Reverend said, lowering his hands. "Please, my friends, don't be sad. You must remember that this is not the end of my life. It is only the beginning. You see, after I climb the tree, I will enter the Owl's world, where there is no pain or sadness. In his world, there is only beauty and love." The Reverend sighed. "I have lived a full life here in the meadow, and I am no longer afraid of what lies ahead of me. I am sorry, my friends, but I must go now. My dear departed wife is up there in The Owl's world, and I don't want to keep her waiting any longer."

When the Reverend finished speaking, he kissed Cat on the forehead and handed me his matchstick cane. "Here, Horatio," the Reverend said, "I don't think I will be needing this where I am going." Then the Reverend smiled and looked back towards the rest of the crowd. "My friends, no matter what happens, always remember to love one another as I have loved you." Then the Reverend turned around and slowly began climbing the Tree of Life.

As the Reverend made his way up the tree, Cat buried her face in her hands and began crying. I reached over to give her a comforting hug, but as the sadness overtook her, she pulled away from me and raced up the center path toward our home in the mulberry bush. I quickly followed her. When we got home, Cat cried herself to sleep and spent most of the day in bed. I didn't know what else to do, so I laid down beside her and nodded off to sleep. When I awoke, it was dark outside, and Cat was gone. I raced outside and found her sitting on a stone and staring towards the Tree of Life. I walked to her, pulled her onto her feet, and hugged her.

"It's okay, Cat, everything is going to be all right," I said, trying to comfort her.

"No it isn't," Cat said and pulled away from me. "I'm getting old just like the Reverend."

"Ahhh, Cat, you're not getting old," I said.

"Yes I am. Don't you understand? It won't be long until I am the one climbing that tree. Then, I will have to say goodbye. I don't ever want to leave you, Jones."

I hugged her again. "Oh, Cat, you have a full life ahead of you. Why are you worrying about this now?"

"Jones, you just don't understand." She pulled away from me and ran. She was crying so hard that she didn't realize where she was going; she was running down the path that led to the home of E. Phil Snake.

When I saw where she was headed, I screamed, "Cat, wait! Don't go that way! Cat, stop! That is where E. Phil Snake lives!" Cat didn't hear me and just kept running. "Cat, you don't understand! E. Phil Snake eats caterpillars!"

Cat continued running, and I ran faster, hoping I could stop her in time. But then something passed between us. It was like a caterpillar, but much bigger and longer. It was the snake. His scaly, black skin reflected the moonlight as he slowly wrapped his body into a circle, completely surrounding Cat. His blood-red eyes stared hungrily at her, and his forked tongue darted in and out of his mouth, wagging menacingly in the night air.

"Ahhhh . . . and what do we have here?" the snake asked.

Cat looked up innocently. "Hello, my name is Cat," she said, wiping the tears from her eyes.

"Funny, you don't look like a cat," E. Phil said as he slowly moved his head down to get a closer look at her. "Cat's are much bigger, and not very tasty, I might add."

As the snake and Cat were talking, I ran toward them as fast as I could.

Goodbye

"Oh, Great Owl of Light, please, I beg you, don't let the snake have her!" I yelled into the sky.

Then I heard the snake again. He spoke in a cold, heartless tone. "Well, hello, Cat. My name is E. Phil Snake, but you may call me Phil. I am so glad that I finally got the chance to eat . . . ha, ha . . . I mean meet you. You know, you really should be a little more careful. Running around out here in the dark all by yourself can be dangerous. I'm sure you know it was curiosity that killed the Cat . . . and it is dinnertime."

The snake began to laugh, an evil laugh that sent a chill down my spine. When I finally reached the snake, my anger was so strong that I just climbed over his body and raced to Cat's side.

"She's not alone!" I screamed. "She's with me!"

E. Phil looked at me, smiled, and then gradually began to tighten the circle that surrounded us.

"Oh look, a buffet!" he hissed.

"Listen, you stupid snake!" I yelled as I pulled Cat behind me. "If all you want is dinner, then let her go and take me instead."

E. Phil thought for a moment and then nodded his head. "You know, that is a very good idea, but here's a better one: I think I will eat you both."

I grew angrier than I had ever been. "That's it!" I yelled. "I don't know who you think you are dealing with, but I am an Adventurer . . . and you will lose!"

E. Phil started laughing, and his tongue danced out of his mouth. "An Adventurer?! Ha-ha-ha, you're no Adventurer. But I will give you credit, you are rather brave, my young friend. It's such a shame that I must eat you. How will I ever live with myself?" E. Phil thought for a moment. "Oh, well, I'll find a way."

The snake pulled back his head, stuck out his fangs, and prepared to strike at us. At that moment, I grabbed Cat, pulled her up onto my back, and ran. I reached the snake's body and started to climb up over it.

"My, my, you are an impressive little climber. Well, let's see if you can climb this."

The snake coiled his body around and added another layer on top of the first one. He was forming a wall, piling one layer of his body on top of another. Every time I climbed over one coil, he would add another. The coils were getting smaller and smaller, forming a cone shape, and Cat and I were trapped inside. It was very hard to climb with Cat hanging onto my back, and I was getting tired.

"Oh, please, Jones, get me out of here. I'm scared, and I just want to go home."

My legs ached, and I was running out of breath. But I struggled to climb higher up the cone-shaped prison the snake had formed around us. My heart pounded, and I gasped for air. I wasn't sure I could get us out of there. I thought about giving up and letting the snake win. But then I thought of Sammy. I thought back to the first day I met him—the day he pinned me to the ground, and I gave up. That was when he'd told me that Adventurers never give up.

"I haven't given up since that day, and I'm not about to start now!" I yelled. I gritted my teeth and pulled myself up over another layer of the snake's body.

When we finally reached the top of the cone, E. Phil added one last coil. Only this time, he wrapped it so tightly around us that Cat and I couldn't even move. We were trapped at the top of the snake's coiled body, and as he tightened his grip, it became harder and harder for us to breathe. Then, suddenly, E. Phil swung his head around right in front of Cat and I. I watched the poisonous venom drip from his fangs as he spoke.

"I don't mean to PRESSURE you, my little friends, but I'm really kind of SQUEEZED for time . . . ha . . . ha," the snake said, laughing.

I felt dizzy as E. Phil's twisted body squeezed the last bit of air out of my lungs. I was terrified and knew if I passed out, he would eat us. But I had to do something to save Cat. Then I got an idea. If I could shoot a line of Traveling Thread into the snake's eyes, he may loosen his grip long enough for us to escape. I reared my head back and shot a long string of Traveling Thread at the snake's eyes. But E. Phil ducked just in time, and I missed! I watched the Traveling Thread soar over the snake's head and fall off in the distance. He was just too fast for me. "Use your head, C.J.," I thought to myself as I gasped for air.

Then I got another idea.

Cat was nearly unconscious and could barely open her eyes. "Cat, wake up! I need you to help me!" I shouted.

"I'm trying, Jones," she said.

I whispered, "On the count of three, spit a line of Traveling Thread at the snake's head. Okay . . . are you ready?"

Cat nodded.

"One . . . Two . . . Three!"

Cat shot a line of thread directly at the snake's head, and when she did, he ducked like I knew he would. Then I nailed him! I shot him right in the eyes with a long piece of Traveling Thread. He was completely blinded, and he went wild. He swung his head back and forth, screaming. His grip loosened and I quickly pulled myself free. I grabbed Cat's hand, but before I could free her, the huge snake tightened his grip again. I pulled her arm as hard as I could, but could not get her out.

"Let her go!" I screamed, pounding my fists on his coiled body.

It was no use, she was trapped. I knew E. Phil would soon get the Traveling Thread out of his eyes.

Goodbye

I had to move fast. I jumped up onto his back and climbed towards his head. E. Phil was still swinging back and forth, so it was difficult to hold on. Each time he swung his head, I crashed from one side of his neck to the other. Pain shot through my body, and my arms felt as though they would be torn off. It hurt so bad that I wanted to let go. "Sammy, where are you?" I thought to myself. If he were here, we would have no trouble beating this stupid snake. But somehow I would have to fight him on my own. So, I gritted my teeth and pulled myself up onto the back of the snake's head. Just then, the Traveling Thread came loose, and the snake could see again. E. Phil immediately reared back, preparing to strike at Cat. When he did, I took several strands of Traveling Thread, swung them over his head, and pulled them into his mouth like a bridle. I held on to the ends of the Traveling Thread, and I pulled back as hard as I could.

You know, you two insects are really beginning to BUG me," the snake mumbled as I tightened my grip.

"I won't let you have her!" I screamed.

"We will see about that," E. Phil hissed around the thread in his mouth and began swinging his head violently.

I held on with all my strength, knowing that if I let go, he would bend down and bite Cat. My fingers started to ache, and my hands were cramping, but there was no way was I going to let go of that thread. Suddenly, E. Phil stopped swinging his head.

"If I can't get to my dinner, I guess I will just have it delivered," he said. "I would like to order one caterpillar please," E. Phil said and his giant tongue darted and wrapped around Cat's body. She pounded on the giant tongue, but it didn't even phase E. Phil, who began pulling Cat toward his mouth.

"Oh look, here it comes now," he said laughing. "Now that's what I call fast food."

"Leave her alone!" I screamed and pounded on his head.

"I'm sorry, my young friend, but I really can't talk right now," he mumbled. "At the moment, Cat's got my tongue."

E. Phil let out a loud hissing laugh that echoed throughout the meadow. I took a chance and quickly flipped myself over his head and slid down his tongue. When I landed beside Cat, I grabbed onto the tongue with both hands and began pulling as hard as I could.

"Pull, Cat, PULL!" I screamed.

Although we were both pulling as hard as we could, we were no match for him. I will never forget the sound of E. Phil's laugh as he pulled us closer and closer. When we reached his mouth, I put my feet up

Goodbye

on his nose for leverage and pulled as hard as I could, but E. Phil just kept pulling us in closer. At that instant, I knew that, no matter how hard I tried, I was not going to be able to save Cat. I also knew that I was a failure as an Adventurer. Then, all of the sudden, the moonlight disappeared, and the shadow of a huge bird fell over us. A thunderous HOOT echoed through the sky. E. Phil stopped pulling and looked up into the darkness. He froze for a second. Then, without saying a word, he let go of Cat, uncoiled his body, and slithered off into the meadow.

Cat and I fell down into the grass below.

"Are you all right, Cat?" I asked as I lifted her into my arms.

"Yes, Jones, I'm fine. I just want to go home."

I carried Cat back to the mulberry bush. She was exhausted, but happy to be alive. Still, I could tell her fear of dying had not disappeared with the snake.

In the days that followed, Cat became more and more tired. Her eyes sagged when she smiled, and her excitement for life was beginning to fade. She tried to hide this from me, but I knew her too well. She was getting old, and her body was growing weaker. Fortunately, Cat was a very strong-willed caterpillar who never let her age stop her from living a full life. She couldn't climb Lover's Landing anymore, and she wouldn't let me help her, so I never asked her to watch a sunset again. I missed watching them, but I knew that if Cat couldn't be there with me, I wouldn't enjoy them anyway. Instead, we took long walks at night and visited friends whenever we could.

One night, while Cat and I were sitting out in the meadow beside the mulberry bush, she began staring down the pathway that led to Lover's Landing. After awhile, she began to cry.

What's the matter, Cat?" I asked.

Cat turned toward me with a sad look on her face and said, "I'm sorry, Jones, I know how much you like to watch the sunsets on top of Lover's Landing, but we will never be able to watch another one together again."

I hugged her. "Oh, Cat, I don't care about watching the sunset," I said. "I'm happy right here in the meadow. It doesn't matter where we are. The only thing that matters is that we are together."

She looked at me with tears in her eyes and smiled. "I love you Jones. I don't believe a word of what you just said, but I love you for saying it."

I sat there holding Cat in my arms and felt a love that I had never known before. But this was to be our last night together.

It was still dark when I woke up the next morning. It was raining, and the wind blew across the meadow, causing a chill in the air.

Goodbye

"Get up, Cat," I whispered.

I turned over to wake Cat up, but she was gone. I jumped up and ran out of the mulberry bush to look for her. The rain hit me in the face as I made my way out into the darkness. I searched for a long time before I finally found her at the foot of the Tree of Life. She was staring up with a look of wonder on her face. She was drenched from head to toe, and the little black dots in her eyes were twice as big as usual.

"Cat, what are you doing out here in the rain?" I asked. "Why don't you come back to bed before you catch a cold."

"I can't go back with you, Jones. I have started my Life Watch."

My heart sank and began filling with tears. "Are you sure, Cat? Maybe this is not your Life Watch. Maybe you just had a bad dream." "It wasn't a bad dream, Jones," Cat said, still staring at the tree. "I dreamed about the Owl . . . oh, it is so beautiful."

"What's so beautiful, Cat?"

"The light," Cat said.

I began to panic. "What light?" I asked.

"The light at the end of the tunnel. It's so beautiful that it is making me feel young again," she said calmly. "It's right there in the tree. Don't you see it?"

I looked at the tree, but I saw nothing.

"No, I don't see anything. C'mon, Cat, let's go," I pleaded. "The rain is coming down pretty hard, and you look like you might be getting sick."

Cat took a deep breath and said, "I'm sorry, Jones, but I can't go back."

My heart started racing, and I began to feel a pain in my chest. "What do you mean you can't go back?!" I yelled. " I don't understand!"

"Jones, I can't explain to you what I am *feeling*, but I will try to explain to you what I am *seeing*." Cat stared deep into the tree. Suddenly, her body jerked forward. Then she said, "It's like I'm being pulled down the tunnel towards a light. I can see memories of my life on the walls of the tunnel."

"What memories?" I asked.

"I am watching us meet for the first time." Cat began laughing. "Jones, you were so cute when you fainted."

I felt Cat's hand touch mine.

"Oh Jones, I'm watching our wedding," she said as tears filled her eyes.

I started to get upset. I wanted to share these memories with her, but no matter how hard I tried, I couldn't see anything.

Then all of the sudden, she screamed. "Oh no, Jones, it's the snake."

"Where? Where's the snake?!" I yelled frantically, looking around and preparing for battle.

Goodbye

I looked in all directions, but E. Phil was nowhere in sight. I didn't understand what was happening. Cat was watching her entire life go by, but her eyes never left the tree. Then she stopped smiling, her mouth dropped open, and her eyes lit up.

"I have reached the light, Jones," Cat said calmly. "I have to go in and face my greatest fear."

"Cat, wait!" I screamed.

"I'm going in now, Jones," she said.

I felt her hand tighten around mine. Then, she stood there in silence for a few moments.

"Cat, are you all right?!" I screamed. "Cat, answer me!"

For the first time that morning, she looked directly into my eyes.

"I think I understand now, Jones," she said peacefully.

"Did you face your fear, Cat?" I asked.

"Yes, I did, Jones," she replied. "It was you."

"Me?" I asked, surprised. "You were afraid of me?"

"No, Jones. I wasn't afraid of you; I was afraid of leaving you. But now I have faced my fear, and I am no longer afraid. I know now that I must move on."

I couldn't believe what I was hearing. "Please, don't leave me, Cat," I begged.

"Jones, I love you, and if I didn't have to, I wouldn't leave. But something is happening to me. I am changing, and I have to go."

"But if you leave, who will take care of me?" I asked, trying to change her mind.

Just then, I heard a familiar voice off in the distance. It was Sammy.

"Hey, what's going on down there? Can't you guys see that it is raining?" Sammy said, coming towards us.

Cat looked at Sammy then back at me. "Jones, I will miss you, and I will be counting the days until we can be together again. But until then, you can take care of yourself." She pulled me close and hugged me tighter than she had ever done before. "Listen, my love, no matter how lonely you get, you must try to enjoy the rest of your life without me; just as I will try to enjoy my new life without you."

Sammy came running up behind me. "Hey, I don't mean to interrupt you guys, but this storm is getting pretty bad. You two should come in out of the rain," he said.

Cat ignored Sammy and kept looking at me. She was trying to say something to me with her eyes, but I couldn't understand what it was. We stood there in silence, holding each other in the pouring rain, until finally she spoke again.

Goodbye

"Jones, it breaks my heart to leave you. But the door is open for me now, and it is time for me to start climbing The Tree."

I realized that I would be spending the rest of my life alone. Just thinking about it made my chest hurt, and I could hardly breathe as the tears continued to fill up my heart. Cat looked at me as if she expected me to say something, but when I didn't, she kissed me and turned to leave. As she turned away, my fear got the best of me, and I reached out and grabbed her arm.

"No, Cat!" I screamed. "Don't go!"

I felt like crying, but for some reason I could not. I had to stop her from leaving.

Trying to pull away from me, Cat said, "Jones, you must try to be strong. Don't you understand . . . "

Cat choked on her words, and the brave look on her face melted into tears. She tried to say more, but all that would come out were sobs.

After a moment, she had enough courage to speak again. "Jones, please, The Owl is calling me home. I've got to go."

I tried to be strong, but when I looked into her tear-filled eyes, I panicked and yelled, "I can't let you!"

The rain had become unbearable, and Cat was getting desperate. Fighting back the tears, she looked over at Sammy and said, "Sammy, please help him."

I felt Sammy's strong hands grab onto my arms, and I heard him say, "You have got to let her go, C.J."

As Sammy pulled me away from her, a flash of jagged light lit up the sky, and an explosion of sound filled my ears. Then there was silence. Fear raced through my entire body. I felt dizzy, and my legs gave out. As I was falling, I felt Sammy catch me. Then everything went black.

When I came to, warm water was falling on my face. Sammy held me in his arms, and Cat was leaning over me.

"Jones," she said, "no matter what happens, you will never be alone, because I love you so much that I won't allow anything to keep us apart for very long. Don't be afraid, Jones. I promise that I will always be with you."

A tear rolled down her cheek and landed on my face. Then she looked at me, kissed me one last time, and began walking towards the tree. Sammy lifted me up in his arms and carried me back to the mulberry bush. Fighting to stay awake, I managed to silently whisper, "Goodbye."

The Point of No Return

Following Cat's death, my days were filled with sadness, but Sammy stood by me and did his best to cheer me up. I don't know what I would have done without him. He told me so many jokes that sometimes I was able to forget my pain. Laughing made me feel better.

Still, without Cat, time passed slowly. The days grew shorter, the nights grew longer, and soon fall came to the meadow. I didn't like this new season; it wasn't warm and rainy like spring, or hot and dry like summer. Fall was cold, and it chilled me to the bone. I spent many nights huddled under my leaf blanket, thinking about Cat. I had promised her that I would try to live a happy life without her, but I was failing. As each day passed, I grew more and more lonely, and I felt my body getting older.

One day, as I was eating my breakfast, I learned that Sammy's wife, Sandy, had started her Life Watch and was climbing the Tree of Life. I jumped up and hurried down the center path to be with Sammy. But by the time I reached the tree, Sammy had already said his goodbyes. Sandy was gone. I walked with Sammy back to the mulberry bush and stayed with him the rest of the day. Sammy was pretty sad, but he told me that he knew that Sandy was in The Owl's world, and this made him feel better. Now Sammy and I were both alone.

Fall continued toward winter and I spent more time on Lover's Landing watching sunsets, alone. One evening, as the sun was setting behind Adventurer Hill, I heard a noise. I looked over at the edge of the stump and saw Sammy struggling to pull his aging body up on top of Lover's Landing. He finally made it up and stood there gasping for air.

I smiled and said, "We're getting old, Sammy."

"I know," he replied. "It took everything I had just to climb up here."

I laughed. "Well, you could always use Traveling Thread."

The Point of No Return

Sammy's old wrinkled face scowled. "Oh, C.J., don't even joke about that. We may be old, but we are still Adventurers."

"I don't know, Sammy, sometimes I wonder if we are getting too old to be Adventurers."

Sammy shook his head and sat down beside me.

"C.J., being an Adventurer is not about rolling down hills or climbing rocks," he said. "It's about believing in yourself and conquering your fears. It's about living life to its fullest."

"Yeah . . . you're right, but it's hard to live life to its fullest without Cat. I miss her, Sammy. I really do. Nothing is the same without her."

I sat there in silence, staring out into the sunset, waiting for Sammy to say something, but he didn't for a long time.

Then he turned to me and asked in a serious tone, "Hey, C.J., I was thinking: if turtles didn't have shells, would they be considered naked or homeless?" Sammy laughed, but I just shook my head. "What? You didn't think that was funny?" he asked.

I knew Sammy was trying to cheer me up, but I was just too sad to laugh.

"What's the matter, C.J.?" he asked.

"I'm sorry, I just don't feel like laughing today. I'm too sad. Actually, I feel like crying, but I can't."

"What do you mean?"

"I can't cry. I have never cried. I didn't even cry when Cat died. The tears filled my heart and I wanted to cry, but I never did. I couldn't. I don't know how."

"You mean you have never cried once in your whole entire life?" Sammy asked, staring at me.

"No," I replied. "I guess the sadness is still inside of me."

Sammy shook his head in amazement. "Boy, I sure cried when Sandy died. I was a mess. It's a good thing you were there to cheer me up, C.J. I don't know what I would have done without you. Thanks."

"It was the least I could do, Sammy. After all, when Cat died, you spent the entire week trying to cheer me up. Heck, you're still trying to cheer me up."

"Yeah, but it's not working," he said. "Hey, wait a minute, I've got one! What do you call a groundhog that runs a lot of errands?" Sammy waited for my answer.

"I don't know, Sammy," I finally said.

"A gopher," he said, laughing hysterically. "You get it? 'Hey, groundhog, GO FOR this, GO FOR that!'"

I just smiled and he said, "C'mon, C.J., that's one of my best jokes. Clarence told it to me a long time ago when he sent me to get him and George some food. I'll never forget how they laughed when I came back carrying all those leaves."

The Point of No Return

I smiled as I thought of the two old Adventurers who had taught us so much. "Yeah," I said, "they used to sit there all day telling jokes and wild stories about their adventures."

"It's kind of weird," Sammy said. "Now that they're gone, it's like they were never even here." He paused. "I wonder if that's going to happen to us?"

"What do you mean?"

"I mean . . . do you think anyone will remember us after we're gone, C.J.? I wish there was some way to leave our mark, you know, so people will know we were here." Sammy shrugged his shoulders and said, "Oh well, it doesn't really matter. I'm going to bed."

Sammy slowly stood up and started for the edge of Lover's Landing. He turned back one last time and looked at me. "Hey, C.J.," he said, smiling. "What do you call the strongest caterpillar in the world?"

"I don't know," I said. "What *do* you call the strongest caterpillar in the world?"

He flexed his muscles and said, "SAMMY!"

This time I laughed, and Sammy smiled with satisfaction before turning away and disappearing over the edge.

"What an amazing friend I have," I thought. "No matter how sad I am, he always finds a way to make me laugh." Sammy was laughing when he left, but I knew he missed Sandy a great deal. I wanted to find a way to cheer him up as he'd done me. Suddenly, the wind picked up, and a giant leaf hit me in the face, giving me an idea. I would make a map of Ponder Rock for Sammy and give it to him as a present. I grabbed the leaf and laid it on the stump. Then, with the pointy end of a stick, I drew a picture of Ponder Rock on the leaf. I labeled all the markers and even added instructions on how to do The Flip. When I finished, I signed the bottom with these words:

In honor of Samson J. Caterpillar, who left his mark on the world by teaching me how to face my fears and believe in myself. He is my best friend and the bravest Adventurer I have ever known. Thank you, Sammy!
Your friend,
Horatio Jones Caterpillar

The map was perfect! I couldn't wait to show it to Sammy. I knew that it would cheer him up. But it was late, and I could barely keep my eyes open. I put my head down to rest, and before I knew it, I had drifted off to sleep.

"Wake up, Jones," a familiar voice whispered. My heart raced with excitement as I realized it was Cat's voice.

The wind whirled all around me, and when I opened my eyes, I was surrounded by a shower of the most beautiful colors imaginable.

The Point of No Return

"Is this a dream?" I thought, wiping the sleep from my eyes. I looked again, but the colors were gone. I was alone. I climbed to my feet and realized that I had fallen asleep on Lover's Landing. Hearing Cat's voice again, even in a dream, made me miss her even more. But then I saw Sammy's map lying beside me, and my sadness turned to excitement.

I rolled up the map, picked up the Reverend's cane—which I was now using as my own—and hobbled off to find Sammy. I finally found him at the base of The Tree of Life. He was staring at it with a strange look in his eyes, a look I thought I had seen before.

I held the map out to him. "Here, Sammy, I have a surprise for you."

Sammy ignored me and continued staring at the tree.

"C.J.," Sammy said in a wavering voice, "I have started my Life Watch."

I began to laugh. "Sammy, you fool me with that one every time."

"I'm not kidding, C.J.," Sammy said very seriously. "The Owl visited me in a dream last night and told me it is time for me to go."

I lowered the map, and my laughter turned to fear when I looked more closely at Sammy's face. He had the same blank stare that I remembered Cat having during her Life Watch. This was not the beginning of one of Sammy's jokes; it was the beginning of something I did not want to happen—not to Sammy, too.

"Oh, C.J., the Life Watch is amazing," Sammy whispered. "You can't begin to imagine what it's like until you experience it yourself. The light at the end of the tunnel makes me feel so young, like I can do anything."

I stood there in silence, listening in amazement at what Sammy was saying.

Sammy went on. "I can see memories of my life on the walls, C.J., and they are so real. I feel like I'm actually reliving them. But it's funny which things I'm remembering. It's not the big things, it's the little things that matter most, C.J."

I felt helpless watching Sammy die. As with Cat, there was nothing I could do to stop it. As his Life Watch progressed, Sammy's mind wandered to other places and different times, but his body never left my side. Then, all of the sudden, he stopped talking and stared deep into the tree, a look of wonder on his face.

"What is it, Sammy?" I asked.

Sammy's eyes widened as he replied, "I'm going into the light now, C.J."

Then I believe Sammy relived his final memory. For, as he stood there, his mouth slowly opened, and his face lit up with a look of understanding.

The Point of No Return

Moments passed, and Sammy turned to me. "I know what is holding me back."

"What, Sammy? What is holding you back?" I asked.

Sammy put his hands on my shoulders, stared deep into my eyes, and said, "C.J., do you remember that time during our first race when I told you that Adventurers must always stick together."

"Yeah, Sammy, I remember," I said.

"Well, I was wrong, C.J. There are times when an Adventurer must stand alone, and this is one of those times."

I started to understand what Sammy was saying and a pain grew in my chest.

"I wish I could stay here with you, because you are my best friend, and I will miss you. But, C.J., it is time for you to stand alone. In my dream, The Owl knew how much I missed Sandy, and he said it was time for us to be together again. I miss her, C.J., and I am giving up my life here in the meadow so I can go up and live with her in the sky." He smiled. "Besides, I have a great joke I can't wait to tell her."

"Why can't I go, too?!" I asked angrily. "I've been away from Cat longer than you have been away from Sandy."

"That is between you and The Owl," Sammy replied. "For some reason, he thinks you're not ready yet."

"How do you know that, Sammy?" I asked.

"Because The Owl told me to give you a message. He said that love is not just about being together, sometimes it is about being apart. He also said that when you learn this, you will find what you are looking for."

"I don't understand!"

"I know, C.J., but maybe when you do understand, you will be ready to climb The Tree."

"I'm ready to climb The Tree now, Sammy, and I'm coming with you!"

Sammy gave me a scowl. "NO, you can't!" he said firmly. "The Owl hasn't called you yet. And you must never take your own life. Life is a gift, and to throw it away before the Owl calls you is the worst mistake you can make. When your time comes, C.J., I promise to meet you on the other side. Until then, you must stay here." Sammy turned back to the tree and gazed into it for a time. "I have to go now, C.J.," he finally said. " . . . so goodbye."

He waited for me to say goodbye, but I just couldn't say it. Sorrow was filling my heart.

"C.J., are you all right?" Sammy asked.

"No," I said. "I couldn't say goodbye to Cat, and now I can't say goodbye to you. I'm afraid. I know that Adventurers aren't supposed to be afraid, but I am. I'm not as strong as you are, Sammy."

The Point of No Return

Sammy looked me in the eyes. "What are you trying to say, C.J.?"

I paused, not wanting to admit it, but I finally told Sammy the truth. "Sammy, I'm not a true Adventurer." I dropped my head.

Without warning, Sammy threw his head back and laughed.

"C.J.," he began and the tone in his voice brought my eyes up to meet his. "You are, without a doubt, the bravest Adventurer I have ever known!"

"So, Horatio Jones Caterpillar, be strong. Straighten up, and give me the Adventurer's death I deserve."

His words pushed their way into my heart, and I felt my fear start to disappear. Sammy always did know what to say to me. I threw out my chest, flung back my head, and stood there as proudly as I could.

Sammy smiled. "That's better!" Then he leaned close and whispered, "Think like an Adventurer, C.J., and we WILL meet again." Then Sammy grabbed onto The Tree of Life and started to climb.

Wanting to cheer him on his way, I yelled, "Hey, Sammy! What do you call the strongest caterpillar in the world?"

I expected him to laugh, but instead, he turned his head to look down at me. A single tear rolled down his cheek.

"I call him my best friend," he said. Then after a moment he continued up The Tree.

"Sammy," I called for the last time. "Tell Cat I miss her."

Without turning, Sammy nodded his head and replied, "I will see you in the light, my friend."

Soon, he was out of sight and I felt as though I had lost everything important in the world. Great pain entered my heart—not from fear or anger, but from loss. I wanted to cry and cry forever, but no tears would come. I just stood there in silence unable to look away from The Tree. I didn't know where to go or what to do. I felt lost! I thought of The Owl and one question burned in my mind: Why wasn't I ready to join Cat and Sammy and Sandy in The Owl's world? If The Owl had the answer, then I wanted to hear it. My anger got the best of me, and I walked to the base of The Tree and began shouting up into The Owl's world.

"I have to talk to you, O Great One!" I yelled. "I want to know why I'm not ready! Do you hear me?! I need to talk to you! I am not a happy caterpillar! Are you listening to me?!"

I waited for The Owl to come down and answer me, but he never came. Suddenly, the wind picked up and blew so hard that it knocked me off my feet and blew Sammy's map out of my hand. Then, just as quickly as the wind had come, it was gone. I climbed back up onto my feet and saw the map had been blown open against the base of the tree. Looking at it, I got an idea.

"Well then, Mr. Owl, if you won't come down to see me, I am coming up to see you!" I screamed up into the sky. "Meet me at the top of Ponder Rock, because I've got a few things I want to say to you."

I grabbed the map, picked up my matchstick cane, and hobbled off toward Ponder Rock. I was determined to talk to The Owl. I didn't want to end my life—Sammy was right, that would be wrong—but I had lived a good long life, and I truly felt that I was ready to start a new one.

When I got to Ponder Rock, I stopped to catch my breath. Resting there, I thought back to that day, so very long ago, when Sammy and I first climbed the great rock. In my mind, I could still hear Sammy's voice coming from marker number two—the stone we called HELLO.

"*Hello, Ponder Rock, my name is Samson J. Caterpillar,*" Sammy's voice echoed from the past. "*And this is my friend Horatio Jones Caterpillar. We are Adventurers! So, prepare to be climbed!*"

I stood there staring at the stone, reliving the memory. Then, again, I heard Sammy's voice in my memory yelling down from marker number three:

"This is where we will say goodbye to the ground and begin our journey into the light."

It seemed like only yesterday that Sammy had stood on that ledge and said those memorable words. Sammy had loved to make speeches, and I had loved to listen to them. He'd been a great speechmaker, but he had been a better friend.

"I wonder where Sammy is right now?" I thought.

"I'm up here, C.J. I found a really neat cave." Again Sammy's voice echoed from the past, and I looked up at marker number four, THE POINT OF NO RETURN, remembering the fear I had felt when I'd stood there for the first time.

"We haven't made it yet, C.J.," the voice in my memory yelled from the top of the curve. *"I already checked it out. The finish line is just a little ways up ahead. C'mon, I will race you to the finish."*

I shifted my eyes to the top of the rock and thought back to how good it felt to do The Flip and then race towards the finish line. The good feelings faded, however, as I looked toward the easy path. Sammy's voice echoed one last time: *"The easy path is for old caterpillars and sissies, not for Adventurers like us."*

"Yes, Sammy," I said, "But we never counted on becoming old Adventurers, ourselves."

I paused for a moment, lowered my head, and hobbled up the easy path toward the top of the rock.

The Point of No Return

When I reached the top, I sat on the edge of the finish line to wait for The Owl. The day wore on, and I became tired of waiting for The Owl. I stood up on my old wobbly knees and walked to the top of the curve. I looked out over the meadow and unrolled Sammy's map and felt sad that he would never see it. Reverently, I began reading the words that were written on the bottom:

In honor of Samson J. Caterpillar, who left his mark on the world by teaching me how to face my fears and believe in myself. He is my best friend and the bravest Adventurer I have ever known. Thank you, Sammy!
                    Your friend,
                    Horatio Jones Caterpillar

I touched the words on the map one last time. Then I let it go and watched it float out across the meadow on the wind.

"Goodbye, my friend," I whispered as the map slowly drifted out of sight.

Then I turned around and went back to the finish line. It took all my strength to pull myself back up. I laid on my back, gasping for air. Before long, I felt my body relax, and I drifted off to sleep.

A thunderous HOOT echoed throughout the meadow and woke me up. It was still afternoon, but the sun was strangely beginning to dim, and the wind was picking up as the darkness deepened. At first I thought a storm was coming and that, maybe, the hoot I had heard was thunder. But the screeching HOOT sounded again, and I knew that this was no storm. The sun winked out, leaving almost total darkness. Then I felt clouds wrap around me and the wind died away. Suddenly, a beam of light from the sky broke through the darkness and shone down on me like a spotlight. I raised a hand to shield my eyes as I looked around, confused. Then a voice from the past spoke inside my head. It was the voice of Reverend Kaleb D. Caterpillar:

It is said that when the world was new, he ruled the skies. He is so beautiful that when the sun saw him, it became jealous and refused to shine while he flew. This is why he only flies at night. But even then, he still glows like a brilliant white light in the darkness.

The Reverend's words sent a chill down my spine. I started shaking and couldn't stop.

"Are you The Great Owl of Light?" I asked, trembling.

The Owl's voice echoed all around me, "Why have you called me here?"

The Point of No Return

I laid there in silence, not knowing what to say, but then I realized that this was my only chance to tell The Owl how I really felt. I took a deep breath and gathered my courage.

"I will tell you why I called you here," I said, trying to be brave. "It's because I want to know why you think I'm not ready to climb The Tree of Life. It isn't fair to leave me here! All my friends are gone, and I am all alone. My heart keeps filling with more and more tears as my friends die, but I still can't cry. I'm so sad inside that my chest hurts." I became angry now. "I miss my friends. I miss Cat. I'm tired of being alone. All I want to do is climb that stupid tree."

The Owl did not reply right away. The silence went on forever it seemed, before The Owl's thunderous voice spoke again.

"SO CLIMB IT!" The Owl boomed.

The wind exploded in my ears, and the darkness disappeared as the late afternoon sun once again lit up the sky. The light was so bright that I had to shut my eyes. When the wind finally died down, I opened my eyes, and The Owl was gone.

"What happened?" I asked myself. Then it hit me. "I must have been dreaming. Yeah, that's it. The loud wind must have startled me awake. . . . Hey, wait a minute . . . that must have been my Owl dream!"

I jumped to my feet, feeling my heart pounding.

It was finally time for me to climb The Tree! The Owl had said so himself. This was the day I had been waiting for a very long time.

"I am coming, Cat!" I yelled as I hobbled down the easy path.

By the time I had reached the bottom of Ponder Rock, the sun had disappeared behind a big dark cloud. It was raining, and I was beginning to feel cold. But none of this mattered to me. I had passed the point of no return, and nothing was going to stop me from getting to that Tree. It rained harder and harder as I made my way down the center path. I trudged on through the mud, and before long, I was standing at the foot of The Tree of Life. My mind wandered as I stared deeper and deeper into The Tree. Then suddenly, The Tree opened up into a long, dark tunnel.

I had started my Life Watch.

The Life Watch

The Life Watch was just as Cat and Sammy had described it. Images from my life lined the walls of the tunnel, and I could see a light shining at the far end. I stared at the light and began to feel young again. My strength was returning. The Reverend had told me that this tunnel actually offered the opportunity to climb into The Owl's world, that when you go into the light, you face your greatest fear. Suddenly, the light blinked. I heard a booming sound, and my body jerked forward. I grew frightened as I thought about what was waiting for me in the light. Then a memory from my past lit up one of the tunnel walls. The scene was so clear that I felt like I was actually there, reliving it. It was Sammy and I on our first rock climb.

"It's not luck, C.J. It's marker number six," Sammy said, hanging upside down from the root at HANGING ON.

Suddenly, my heart swelled with excitement and all I wanted was to follow Sammy up that rock. But then the light blinked again, and I was pulled forward out of that memory and into a new one. My heart leapt when I heard the familiar voice of the Reverend Kaleb D. Caterpillar and then saw him on another wall of the tunnel.

"You may now kiss the bride," the Reverend said.

I watched as Cat and I jumped from the top of Ponder Rock. We twirled around each other until the fall brought us together. I hadn't seen Cat since her death, and just looking at her made me feel happy. She was so beautiful that I couldn't help staring at her, but soon the light blinked and pulled me further down the tunnel, the image fading behind me. On and on I traveled, viewing scene after scene from my life. The memories on the walls passed by very quickly, and it was wonderful to watch Cat and I grow old together. For the first time since she had died, I felt happy. However, I knew this feeling wouldn't last, for fear was growing inside of me as I moved closer to the light. Then I heard something that sent a chill down my spine: the icy laughter of E. Phil Snake.

"Ha-ha-ha, you're no Adventurer," E. Phil said to me from the tunnel wall. But the snake was not what I feared most, it was the memory waiting for me in the light. The light was blinking faster now, and the booming sound was so loud my ears hurt. I pushed my body against the tunnel walls, trying to stop myself, but the light's power was just too strong. It continued drawing me down the tunnel. Fear flooded through me as the light blinked faster and faster. Now I was traveling with tremendous speed, heading straight into the center of the light. Just as I was about to go into it, I screamed "No!"

Suddenly, a memory of the Reverend Kaleb D. Caterpillar appeared on the wall to my left.

"You must overcome your worst fear," the Reverend said to me from the past. And though his voice was reassuring, my heart raced as the Reverend spoke. *"When you go into the light, you will see a memory, a memory of something that scared you more than anything else. When you can relive that memory without being afraid, then, and only then, will you be allowed to climb the Tree of Life and enter The Owl's world."*

I was more scared than I'd ever been in my life, but I knew that to be with Cat again, I had to go into the light and face my worst fear. So, I gathered up all my courage, closed my eyes, and stepped into the light. It was warm and bright inside the light, and when I finally found the strength to open my eyes, the first thing I saw was Cat. I was holding her in my arms, and it was wonderful. We were at the base of the Tree of Life, and Sammy was standing behind me. I realized that this was a memory of Cat's Life Watch. We stood there in silence, holding each other in the pouring rain, until finally she spoke.

"Jones, it breaks my heart to leave you. But the door is open for me now, and it is time for me to start climbing The Tree."

Cat looked at me as if she was expecting me to say something, but when I didn't, she kissed me and turned to leave. As she turned around, my fear got the best of me, and I reached out and grabbed her arm.

"Oh no, Cat, I can't go through this again. I have spent so much time trying to forget this moment."

Trying to pull away from me, Cat said, "Jones, you must try to be strong. Don't you understand . . . "

Cat choked on her words, and the brave look on her face melted into tears. She tried to say more, but all that would come out were sobs.

After a moment, she had enough courage to speak again. "Jones, please, the Owl is calling me home. I've got to go."

The Life Watch

I shook my head no as I looked into her tear-stained eyes. I panicked. "No, I can't do it, Cat. I can't let you go. I love you too much."

The rain had become unbearable, and Cat was getting desperate. Fighting back the tears, she looked over at Sammy and said, "Sammy, please help him."

I felt Sammy's strong hands grab onto my arms, and I heard him say, "You have got to let her go, C.J."

As Sammy pulled me away from her, a flash of jagged light lit up the sky, and an explosion of sound filled me ears. There was silence. Suddenly, fear raced through my entire body. I felt dizzy, and my legs gave out. As I was falling, I felt Sammy catch me. Then, everything went black.

The next thing I knew, I was back at the Tree of Life. Cat and Sammy were gone. The tunnel was gone. And all those terrible memories were gone, too. It was early evening. The rain had slowed a little, and my Life Watch was over. I had failed. When I realized this, my sorrow turned to anger.

"Why?!" I screamed. "Why did I fail?! I don't understand! What did I do wrong?!"

I was tired of playing this game. And since The Owl himself had told me that I could climb The Tree, I was not going to let some stupid Life Watch keep me from being with Cat. I walked over to the base of The Tree and began yelling up into the branches.

"Listen to me, Tree of Life! I'm coming up there, so prepare to be climbed!" I broke the Reverend's cane across my knee and threw it to the ground. "I don't think I will be needing this where I am going!" I screamed.

I said goodbye to the ground forever and started climbing up towards the beginning of a new life.

It didn't take long to realize that climbing the Tree of Life would be a difficult task. It was straight up, and the bark was deeply cracked and grooved. Even Travelling Thread was of no use. I climbed all evening, through the rain, and even though my anger had given me strength, I was growing very tired. The sun had gone down, bringing darkness and cold. My hands and legs grew numb. It took all my strength to keep climbing. I looked desperately for a place to rest, but I couldn't find one. I began to worry that I wasn't going to make it. Then, just as my legs were about to give out, I saw it: a hole in The Tree up ahead. It looked like a perfect place to rest. I climbed toward it as quickly as I could, and was about to pull myself in when an old, brown chipmunk reached out and tugged on my chin.

"Hey, worm, why the long face?" he said and began laughing hysterically.

"Who are you?" I asked.

"I'm Peety, Peety The Chipmunk. Who are you?"

The Life Watch

"My name is C.J.," I said, shivering.

"Nice to meet you, C.J.," he said and pulled me into the cave. "I do feel, however, that it is my duty to inform you that it is raining outside. Perhaps this isn't the best time to be climbing The Tree. Now, if it were sunny out, that would be a good time to climb a tree. But it's not sunny out. So, in my opinion . . . "

Peety rambled on, and I thought he was a little strange. He moved and spoke very quickly, and he didn't make much sense. It was warm inside the hole, though, and I could feel my strength quickly returning. Soon, my thoughts returned to Cat, and I wanted to continue my climb.

"Listen, Peety," I interrupted him. "I've got to go. I have to meet The Great Owl of Light."

Peety continued to ramble as though he hadn't heard me, so I began pulling myself out of the cave.

"Oh, okay," Peety said. "You're going up to see The Owl. Well, that's good. I'll see you late . . . HUH!! . . . "

Peety gasped, then shuddered. He shook his head back and forth like someone had just hit him. "Crimeney sakes!!!! You're gonna do what?" He grabbed my legs and yanked me back into the hole.

"Wha . . . wha . . . why on earth would you want to do that? I can't imagine why anybody would WANT to go up and see The Owl!" Peety exclaimed.

"Because my wife is up there," I replied. "And I want to be with her again."

"Oh, I get it. You're afraid of being alone," Peety said.

"No, I'm not!" I shot back. "I just want to be with my wife, and I want to see my friends again!"

Peety scratched his head and thought for a moment. "Hmmm. Well, I'm afraid I have some bad news for you then. The rain washed out the path. So, there is no way to get up there. There used to be a path, but now there is not. It's gone. The rain washed it away. So like I said—"

I grabbed Peety's toes in frustration and shook them. "What do you mean there is no way up there?!"

Peety pulled away and went to the edge of the hole. "Come see for yourself," he said and pointed to the top of The Tree. I followed his finger and saw a line around The Tree where the bark ended. Above the line, there was nothing but a smooth hard surface.

"Where the bark ends and the smooth surface begins," Peety explained, "is the beginning of The Owl's territory. You see, The Owl clawed all the bark off the top of The Tree to keep other animals like us from getting up there. Now, that smooth surface is impossible to climb. Believe me, I've tried. You just slip and slide, and the next thing you know, you find yourself lying on the ground with a horrible backache.

Of course, because you're such a little fellow, a fall like that would probably—"

"Peety," I interrupted, "there's got to be a way to get up there."

"Well, normally there is," Peety went on to explain. "There is usually a path that leads up around the back of The Tree and takes you right up to the top. But, unfortunately, with all this rain, the path is just too slick. So, there is no way to get up there. There used to be a path, but now it can't be climbed. The rain made it too slippery." Peety stopped and shook his head. "Wait a minute . . . did I say that already? Oh well, it doesn't matter. Sometimes I repeat myself. I don't think I repeat myself, but some people say I repeat myself. I wonder why they think I repeat myself. Oh, it doesn't matter. You see, there used to be a path, but with all this rain—"

"No, Peety!" I yelled. "You don't understand! I've got to get up there! You've got to help me find a way! I have to see Cat!"

Peety thought for a moment, rubbing his chin. "Hmmmm . . . no . . . no . . . nope . . . no, I'm sorry, there is no way to get up there. You would think there would be, but there's not. And I should know, I live in The Tree. I would like to help you, but I can't. There is absolutely, positively, without a doubt, no other way to get up there! . . . Well, there is one way:

Lightning Limb. I guess I should have thought of that before."

I felt a ray of hope. "Where is Lightning Limb, Peety?"

"It's right up there," Peety said, pointing to the stump of an old limb. "It used to be like the other limbs of The Tree, but it was struck by lightning a long time ago, and part of it fell off. Now, all that is left is that short stump that sticks out from The Tree right where the bark ends. The bottom of the stump still has bark on it, but the top is completely smooth. Normally, I would have told you that you'd be crazy to climb it. But not to long ago this crazy orange and white worm showed up and did just that. It was the most amazing thing I have ever seen. He just—"

"Orange and white worm?" I asked. "Do you mean, Sammy?"

"Yeah, Sammy, that was his name," Peety said. "Do you know him?"

"Yeah, I know him. He's my best friend."

Peety rolled his eyes and said, "Well, your best friend is nuts! I tried to tell him how dangerous it was, but he wouldn't listen to me. He just laughed and said, 'I've climbed rocks tougher than that.' He said that it reminded him of some place called Powder Rock, Pain Rock, something like that. Anyway—"

The Life Watch

"You mean, Ponder Rock?" I asked anxiously.

"Yeah, that was it. Ponder Rock," Peety answered. "You know, it was the funniest thing. The path was perfectly fine before the rain came, but for some reason, he was determined to climb Lightning Limb. I don't know why he did it, but he did it!"

"Because he is an Adventurer, that's why," I said proudly.

Peety sighed. "Well, whatever . . . You know, it was amazing how well that worm could climb. He was the bravest worm I've ever seen. He crawled up to the base of the stump, bent his body backwards, and started crawling upside down underneath it."

"That's just like marker number five on Ponder Rock, THE LIFE WATCH," I thought to myself as Peety continued to speak.

"Then he did something truly amazing. When he reached the end of the limb, he began swinging his body back and forth." Peety began swinging his head back and forth as if he were watching Sammy in his mind. "Then do you know what he did? The crazy worm let go. Crimeney sakes! I thought he was going to fall, but he didn't. He just flung his whole body up in the air, did a somersault, and landed right on top of the limb. I have never seen anything like it."

"I have," I said smiling. "It's called The Flip."

Peety just ignored me and said, "Then, after he was on top, he looked back at me and yelled, 'I will see you in the light, my friend.'" Peety paused, a confused look on his face. "What do you suppose that means?"

"That means I can climb Lightning Limb," I answered.

Peety shook his head. "I don't know. It wasn't raining when your friend climbed it. It is much too dangerous to climb it right now. I feel that it is my duty to absolutely forbid you to climb that limb tonight. Maybe you should stay here for the night and try to climb it in the morning. I mean, after all, as the old saying goes, 'the early worm gets the bird.'" Peety shriveled up his brow. "Wait a minute, that's not right. It's 'the early bird that's worth two in the bush.' No, that's not it, but it's something like . . . um . . . if you are a bird or a worm, you've got to get up early. I don't know why they have to get up early. I hate getting . . . "

As Peety rambled on, I climbed out of the hole. Apparently, Peety didn't realize I had left because I could still hear him talking as I made my way up The Tree.

After only a few minutes in the cold rain, I was miserable again. My body was soaking wet, and I was freezing cold. I kept climbing, though, despite the pouring rain, until I reached the stump that Peety called Lightning Limb. I believed that this was the one thing standing between me and Cat. So, I reached deep inside myself and found strength I didn't know I had.

The base of the stump looked just like Ponder Rock. I knew that if Sammy could climb it, then I could, too. The rain started falling faster and beating down on me so hard that I had trouble breathing. I stood there, staring at Lightning Limb and watching the water flow down its sides like two giant waterfalls. There was only a narrow strip of bark underneath the limb that was still dry. Suddenly, I wasn't sure I could make it, because when Sammy had climbed Lightning Limb he hadn't had to worry about being knocked off by the water. I was frozen with fear, but then I thought about Cat and kept moving.

Taking a deep breath, I bent backwards and pulled myself up onto the thin strip of dry bark underneath the stump. I told myself that this was just like climbing through THE LIFE WATCH on Ponder Rock. I carefully crawled along the bottom of the limb as the rain flowed down and formed two giant walls of water on each side of me. I knew if I moved one inch to my left or right, the water would catch me and drag me down. I crawled, one step at a time, until I reached the end of the stump. My fingers burned from the incredible cold, and my back ached so bad that it hurt to breathe.

I hung there frozen stiff, thinking about what I had to do next. Just like LETTING GO on Ponder Rock, I would have to flip my body up into the air and catch the top of the stump. I wished Sammy were up there waiting to catch me, just like the old days, but he wasn't. I was alone! Water splashed onto my fur and made me heavy. I couldn't hold on much longer. I had to act fast. I swung my body back and forth, but the rain began pouring down over the end of the stump. Every time I swung out, a freezing blast of water hit me in the face. I couldn't see, and I was losing my grip. I didn't think there was any way I could make The Flip in this rain.

"Maybe I should try tomorrow," I thought. "Peety was right. I'll come back tomorrow. I'll be able to make The Flip easily when it's not raining."

I stopped swinging and started crawling backwards, but the waterfalls had closed in together, and the thin strip of dry bark behind me was gone. Then the water started flowing toward me. I was trapped and running out of time!

Distantly, I heard Peety rambling on down below. "Peety, help me!" I screamed.

It was no use. Peety couldn't hear me over the roar of the water. Then it dawned on me—Traveling Thread. I could use Traveling Thread to climb to the top of the stump. It would be like quitting—real

The Life Watch

Adventurers don't use Traveling Thread—but as the water closed in on me, I realized I had no choice. But before I could act, a surge of water hit me and began dragging me off the limb. I held on as tightly as I could, but the water was too forceful.

"All right, that's it! I give up!" I screamed and shot a piece of Traveling Thread up to the top of the stump.

I pulled myself out of the water, one thought already haunting me: a true Adventurer would not have used Traveling Thread. I was not a true Adventurer, and I never would be. What Sammy had accomplished in just a few days, I could not accomplish in an entire lifetime. I was a failure. I dragged myself to the top of the limb and laid there in shame. But then I noticed something strange about the limb, it was not as smooth as I thought it would be. Its cracked and dried skin actually felt warm under my feet. I looked more closely and was shocked to discover I had crawled onto the claw of a large bird. And when I heard its thunderous HOOT echo in my ears, I knew that I had entered the world of The Great Owl of Light!

Hanging On

My jaw dropped open in awe as I looked up into the face of the creator of the meadow. The Great Owl of Light was larger than I had ever imagined. My legs started to shake and my lips to tremble. No matter how hard I tried, I couldn't catch my breath. The Owl's monstrous head suddenly swooped down and stopped directly in front of me. His eyes looked right through me, and his bloodstained beak made me fear for my life. Just then, I heard Peety yelling from below.

"Hey, worm, I finally figured it out! It's 'the early bird gets the worm.' See, I knew that if I just put my mind to it, I would eventually figure it . . . huh . . .

Hanging On

Crimeney sakes! The early bird gets the worm . . . Hey, worm, be careful!!"

The Owl pulled back and spread his huge wings. He stuck out his chest, threw his head back, and opened his razor sharp beak. "He is really going to eat me," I thought. I put my arm up, trying to protect myself, when all of the sudden, he yawned.

"Haughhhhh! . . . Sorry, caterpillar, I didn't get much sleep today. I'm still a little tired, so you will have to excuse me." He stretched his wings and yawned again.

I was relieved that The Owl wasn't going to eat me. My fear faded, and The Owl smiled as he tucked his wings behind him.

"Welcome to my home, Horatio. I'm glad you finally made it."

I began to forget all of the pain from the past; I had made it to The Owl's world. I knew that it wouldn't be long before I could be with Cat again. I was just about to ask The Owl where she was, when he leaned down, looked into my eyes, and said, "Get on."

"What?" I asked, confused.

"Get on my back," The Owl said. "We are going night flying."

I didn't know what flying was and my knees started to shake again. The Owl saw my fear and explained that flying is when you ride on the wind.

He also told me that the wind would take us anywhere we wanted to go, but only if we were nice to it.

I was still reluctant because I had never ridden on the wind before.

"Listen, Horatio," The Owl said. "The wind doesn't let just anyone ride on it, and neither do I. So, are you coming or not?" He gave me a questioning look.

It had stopped raining, and the storm clouds were drifting away. The Owl ruffled his wings to shake off the rain, and the sight of it was so beautiful and graceful that I just stood there staring and wishing I had wings. He was white from the top of his head to the tip of his tail, and when the last of the clouds fled the sky, the moon shone on him and he lit up the night. I climbed onto his back, grabbed the feathers behind his neck, and buried myself in them. The feathers formed a blanket of warmth that surrounded my entire body. For the first time in a long while, I felt safe.

Then The Owl sprang from the branch. He stretched out his wings and the wind rushed underneath them, lifting us upward. We flew in silence for a long time, but I remained tucked inside the warm feathers. Finally, my curiosity got the best of me. I poked my head up, and felt a freedom I had never felt before. The wind blew through my fur, and I tasted the cool rain on my lips. I heard the flapping of the

Owl's mighty wings, and I could see the moon glistening up above. It was beautiful.

"How do you like flying, Horatio?" The Owl asked.

"It's great," I said, smiling. "I wish I could fly."

The Owl smiled back and said, "Never stop dreaming, Horatio, because you never know when your dreams will come true."

I wanted to ask him where we were going, but even though I really liked The Owl, I wasn't brave enough to question the creator of the meadow. Before long, my face got cold, so I ducked back into the warm feathers.

"Listen up, Horatio," The Owl said. "I'm going to tell you a story. Once upon a time, when I was just a small owlet, my father tried to teach me how to fly, but I refused to learn. I was so afraid of falling that I decided I was never going to leave the nest. Since all my brothers and sisters had already gone, I was the only one left. But I thought I was perfectly happy where I was. Then one day, my father picked me up by the back of my neck and carried me to the edge of the limb. He took off, holding me in one large talon. As we flew, I told him I wanted to go home, but he wouldn't listen. He just kept showing me how to fly. I didn't want to learn, so I didn't pay attention to him. All I could think about was going back to the nest. Then my father said something to me that I will never forget. He said, 'The secret of flying is that, if you cannot glide, your wings are too wide.' Then, without warning, my father did something I never dreamed he would do. He let go! I plunged toward the ground, and I was so scared. My body tumbled end over end through the sky, and I knew I was about to smash into the ground. But then something wonderful happened: my wings came to life and opened. They stopped my tumbling, but I still didn't know how to use them, and I continued plummeting faster and faster toward the ground. Then, my father's words raced through my mind: 'If you cannot glide, your wings are too wide.' So, I pulled my wings in a little and pushed them forward, and suddenly I started to glide. It was the greatest feeling I had ever felt, and I have been flying ever since. You see, Horatio, my father's love helped me overcome my fears. He knew what was best for me, and he taught me what I needed to know to achieve it. Horatio, you must realize that love is stronger than fear. It will give you strength to overcome anything, even yourself."

When The Owl finished his story, I was confused. I wasn't sure why he had told it to me.

"So what did you think of my story, Horatio?" The Owl said and looked back at me again.

"I liked it," I said. "Is that the end?"

Hanging On

"Yep. That is the end of the story, and it is also the end of our flight."

I was surprised to see we were landing back on top of Lightning Limb. I climbed down off The Owl's neck and onto a nearby branch, but I was still a little confused by his story.

"Well, it's been nice talking to you, Horatio," The Owl said as he turned to leave. "But I've got to get something to eat before sunrise. I'll see you later."

"Hey, wait a minute!" I yelled. "What's going on?! Where are you going?!"

The Owl blinked. "I just told you," he said. "I am going to get something to eat."

"Well, what am I supposed to do now?" I asked as I looked around. "Where is everybody? Where's Cat? Where's Sammy?"

The Owl shrugged his shoulders. "I guess they've already moved on."

"To where?" I asked anxiously.

"I imagine they went to live in the sky," The Owl said.

"Isn't this the sky?" I asked.

"No," The Owl said. "This is a tree."

I started to panic. Why wasn't The Owl helping me find my friends?

"Then I want to go live in the sky, too," I demanded.

The Owl looked at me very seriously. "You can't."

"Why not?" I demanded.

"I don't know. I guess you're not ready yet," The Owl replied.

"Why am I not ready?"

The Owl shrugged his shoulders. "There's probably something that you still have to learn."

"What . . . what do I have to learn?" I asked, trembling. I was beginning to think I would never see Cat again.

"I don't know. Listen, Horatio, I've got to go. I'm getting hungry."

"What do you mean you don't know!" I asked in desperation. "Aren't you the creator of the meadow?!"

The Owl shook his head. "Listen, Horatio, I might as well let you in on a little secret. I am not the creator of the meadow."

My heart sank.

"You're not?!" I asked.

The Owl straightened his feathers and continued. "No, the creator of the meadow is much more beautiful and wise than I could ever be. She is very gentle and yet very powerful. She is the mother of change, and her name is Nature. I did not create this meadow; Mother Nature did. I'm just one of her helpers. I watch over it for her."

I stared blankly at The Owl as the rain poured down on me. All my life I had been told The Owl was the creator of the meadow. Now he was telling that somebody's mother created it and that her name was Nature. I was soaking wet, and I was losing hope. The Owl walked to the edge of Lightning Limb and began preparing for flight.

"It's been nice talking to you, Horatio, but I really have to go."

"Hold on!" I screamed. "You can't just leave me here by myself."

The Owl swiveled his head to look at me. "Listen, Horatio, Mother Nature always knows what's right. When you learn to let go and trust her power, the changes in your life will not be so hard."

"But wait . . . I'll freeze out here," I yelled, becoming desperate.

The Owl just winked and said, "Don't worry, Horatio, you'll think of something."

Then, with one last smile, The Owl leapt into the sky. The wind from his great wings blew me off my branch. I tried to imitate The Owl by flapping my arms wildly, but of course I continued falling. Out of instinct, I shot a line of Traveling Thread at the branch I fell from. I bit down on the thread and instantly stopped my fall. I hung there, dangling back and forth in the cold wind. I shivered uncontrollably, and I knew I had to get back to the branch and find some-place to get warm. I tried pulling myself up by the

Traveling Thread, but it was too far and my arms were too tired. Pretty soon, my legs started to grow numb from the cold. I was running out of time, and I had to think of something fast.

"Maybe I can weave a blanket of Traveling Thread and wrap it around me," I thought. "That should keep me warm." I got to work, starting at my feet and working my way up. I was half way done with my blanket when I saw The Owl fly directly beneath me.

"See, Horatio, I knew you would think of something."

I wanted to talk to The Owl, but he flew away again and I went back to weaving my Traveling Thread blanket. With each new layer, I felt warmer, and by the time I reached my neck, the numbness in my body was gone. Just before I finished my blanket, the rain stopped, but it was still as cold as ever outside. I looked around one last time, took a deep breath, and sealed myself in. It was warm inside my Traveling Thread blanket, and I knew I was going to make it through the night. Even though my life seemed hopeless, I was still hanging on!

Letting Go

Snuggled within my blanket I got warmer and warmer. I thought about Cat, knowing she was in The Owl's world somewhere, and I hoped she was warm like me. In my heart, I felt she was fine and I relaxed. I grew very sleepy and was about to drift off when I saw something I had never seen before. It seemed the clouds were breaking apart and falling to the ground, and I knew my world was coming to an end. But the gently falling flakes were pretty to watch, and they soothed me to sleep.

That night I dreamed of a white world that was so cold it made me shiver in my silk blanket. My dream seemed to last forever, but when it finally ended, I began to feel warm. I heard the sound of water dripping and the chirping of baby birds in the distance. Then something frightening happened. I found myself standing at the beginning of the Life Watch tunnel again.

"Oh no! Why am I here again?!" I yelled.

I wasn't expecting anyone to answer me, but a memory of Clarence appeared on the wall of the tunnel. It was a memory of the first day I met him.

"Because you need to face your fear that's why," Clarence said from the past.

"What am I afraid of?!" I screamed.

Then a memory of Peety The Chipmunk spoke to me from the other tunnel wall. *"You're afraid of being alone,"* Peety muttered.

"Of course I am!" I shouted. "What if I never see Cat again?!"

Then I watched a memory of my own wedding and heard the Reverend Kaleb D. Caterpillar say, *"You must trust that your love will bring you together."*

I sighed. "I'm trying to believe that . . . I really am. But I can't. I'm afraid."

Suddenly, I heard the voice of The Great Owl of Light from the other tunnel wall. *"Horatio, you must realize that love is stronger than fear. It will give you strength to overcome anything, even yourself."*

Letting Go

The light appeared at the end of the tunnel, and I was being pulled into it. I would have to face my greatest fear once and for all. There was nothing I could do to prevent it. I lowered my head and whispered, "All right, I hope I'm ready."

I was still afraid I wouldn't be able to face my fear, but when I thought about sitting with Cat and watching the sunset, I decided to ask one more time. "What do I have to do to make it through this time?"

A memory of Cat's Life Watch rose on the tunnel wall, and I heard Sammy say, *"You have got to let her go, C.J.!"*

"But why, Sammy? That's what I don't understand!" I said, shaking my head. "Why do I have to let her go?"

This time it was Cat who answered. *"Because, Jones, if you don't, then the tears will fill up your heart, and you will carry that sadness around inside of you forever."* It was the memory of when she had explained to me how to cry. I looked at her face and knew once again that she was the most beautiful creature in the world.

The image of Cat faded, and I turned and stared directly into the light. I did not want to go inside, but I had no choice. So, I closed my eyes and surrendered to it. I fell into the light and once again found myself standing at the foot of the Tree of Life, reliving Cat's

:ld Cat in my arms, and Sammy was
1 me. We remained there in silence,
ther in the pouring rain, until finally

*Jones,   breaks my heart to leave you. But the
door is open for me now, and it is time for me to start
climbing The Tree."*

My heart was full of tears, and it was now so heavy
that it seemed to be slowing down. I could barely
breathe. Cat looked at me as if she expected me to say
something, but when I didn't, she kissed me and turned
to leave. As she turned away, my fear got the best of
me, and I reached out and grabbed her arm.

"Wait, Cat, don't go. There is something I need to
say to you."

*"Jones, you must be strong. Don't you understand
. . ." Cat choked on her words, and the brave look on
her face melted into tears. She tried to say more, but
all that would come out were sobs.*

After a moment, she was able to speak again. *"Jones,
please, the Owl is calling me home. I've got to go."*

I looked into her tear-stained eyes and said, "I
know. I love you, Cat. I loved you enough to die for
you. But since then, my love has grown, and now I
love you enough to live for you."

*Fighting back the tears, she looked over at Sammy
and said, "Sammy, please help him."*

Letting Go

I felt Sammy's strong hands grab onto my arms, and I heard him say, "You have got to let her go, C.J."

Then I realized what I had to do. I slowly pulled away from him and said, "I know I do, Sammy, but this time I must do it for myself."

As soon as I said this, the scene changed. Sammy disappeared. I was confused, but I looked back at Cat and forgot about everything else. It was wonderful to hold her again if only for a moment.

"Cat, I know you can't really hear me, because you're just a memory, but I want you to know I love you. And no matter what happens, my love will never change. I know that if you go my life will be empty. But I love you more than my life, Cat, and this is why I am letting you go now."

Then I kissed her one last time, hugged her as tightly as I could, and let her go. As I watched Cat climb up out of my life, I felt the tears in my heart begin to overflow and rise from my chest. My bottom lip quivered, and I whispered, "Goodbye." I could taste the sadness in my throat as a single tear ran down my cheek.

The Tree disappeared, and I found myself back inside my silk blanket. I was sadder than I had ever been, and for the first time in my life, I was crying. One after another, tears rolled off my face, over my shoulders, and down my back. I cried so hard that I

ne wrinkles on my face melting away, and
feel young again. After awhile, the tears on
k began to dry, and as they did, they hardened
racked. When I moved, these solid tears moved
with me.

My chest felt lighter, for the heavy sadness in my heart had spilled out of my eyes and had become a part of me. My body was weak, but my spirit was strong. Free of the tears, my heart began beating faster. It pumped life into the solid tears hanging from my back. I could feel them growing, but in my silk blanket I couldn't see them. I grew stronger, and I realized that I was not dying, I was changing and growing. Soon, the dried tears on my back were too big for the blanket, and it began to rip. A thought occurred to me: "She is out there. Cat is waiting for me." Just thinking about the possibility of seeing Cat made my heart race. The beating of my heart became louder and louder; I could hear nothing else. Then there was silence. In one brief moment, I made the decision to live.

I screamed, "I love you, Cat!" and exploded out of my blanket!

A Dream Come True

Once I was free, I fell quickly towards the ground. I tried to stop myself by shooting a line of Traveling Thread up to the branch like I had done before, but nothing came out! I tried to spit again, but still no thread came out! I should have been afraid, but I wasn't. My heart was healed, and I was free. "I am not dead!" I thought to myself. "I'm alive!"

Then, amazingly, the solid tears on my back came to life and spread out. They had become big beautiful wings! My life as a caterpillar was over, and I had become something else, something much better. Just like The Owl, I had wings and could fly. That's when

125

I realized why The Owl had told me the story about flying. Just as I was about to hit the ground, his words raced through my mind: *"If you cannot glide, your wings are too wide."*

So, I narrowed my new wings, pushed them forward, and started gliding. With each flap of my wings, I climbed higher and higher back into the sky.

"Wow! I made it!" I screamed.

Suddenly, something hit me and knocked me out of control. It pinned my arms and tangled my wings. I tried to break free to regain my balance, but no matter how hard I tried, I couldn't. My heart pounded as I fell through the air. But then, suddenly, whatever was tangled in my wings loosened its grip, and I was able to fly free. I quickly turned to see what had hit me, and found myself staring directly into the eyes of Samson J. Caterpillar. Only now, he did not look like a caterpillar. He had huge orange and black wings and two black antennae on the top of his head. He looked much younger, but I knew it was Sammy.

"Sammy!" I screamed.

I was so excited to see my old friend that I stopped paying attention to what I was doing and flew head first into a tree branch. THUD! I was out cold! When I finally came to, I was lying on the ground. Sammy was hovering over me, prying my eyelids open.

A Dream Come True

"Boy, that's using your head, C.J.!" Sammy said, laughing hysterically.

I felt dizzy. "Sammy, what happened?" I asked, rubbing my head.

"You did it, C.J., you faced your greatest fear. You finally made it into The Owl's world."

I was confused. "What do you mean, Sammy? This isn't The Owl's world. We're still in the meadow. Look, there is the Tree of Life, and over there is Ponder Rock."

Sammy pointed up to the sky. "The Owl's world is up there, C.J., and those new wings of yours give you the key to enter that world any time you want."

My heart raced. Ever since Cat's death, I had been dreaming of this moment, and now it was finally here. Before I even realized what I was doing, I flew straight up into the air.

"I made it! I made it!" I screamed. "I'm finally going to see Cat again, and nothing can stop me now."

THUD! I flew headfirst into the same tree branch. I was out cold . . . again. When I came to, Sammy was laughing so hard that he could barely even speak.

"C.J., this is no time to sleep," he said as he flew into the air.

Sammy's laugh reminded me of the old days. I thought about climbing Ponder Rock and the other adventures we had shared. I thought about my old life as a caterpillar, and then I thought about Cat.

"Sammy, have you seen Cat?" I asked anxiously.

"Yes, I have seen her, C.J.," Sammy said, "but she is pretty far away."

"Why isn't she here waiting for me?"

"C.J., listen. You have come a long way, but your journey is not over. You still have a ways to go. So, come on. You've earned your wings, and now it's time to use them."

"Where are we going?"

"To a Mud Puddle meeting."

Sammy flew away. I leapt up into the air and followed after him. We flew past the Tree of Life and headed out of the meadow, which gave me a strange feeling. I had never left the meadow before. But I was doing a lot of things that I had never done before. Being a butterfly was wonderful. I felt young again, and flying was more fun than I could have ever imagined. I didn't know what a Mud Puddle meeting was, but I couldn't wait to get there. Sammy said that all the other butterflies would be there, and I hoped that Cat would be one of them.

Soon, the Mud Puddle came into view. From the air, it looked just like a raindrop on the ground. But as we got closer, I realized that it was much bigger than I thought. We landed next to it, and the other butterflies greeted us. One of them, a beautiful pink and white butterfly, came up to Sammy and kissed him. It was his wife, Sandy.

"Hey, look who I flew into," Sammy said to her.

"Hello, C.J.," Sandy said. "I'm glad you finally made it. You are all that Sammy has been talking about for the last few days."

"Hello, Sandy," I said. "It's great to see you again. I missed you all so much. Have you seen Cat? Is she here?"

Sandy shook her head. "No, I'm sorry, C.J. I haven't seen her. But don't worry, I'm sure she is around here somewhere."

I looked around, but Cat was nowhere in sight. My excitement faded, and I was beginning to feel frustrated. It was nice to see Sammy and Sandy again, but I felt lonely and a little awkward without Cat. Soon, two other butterflies flew our way. As they approached, I recognized one of them. It was the Reverend Kaleb D. Caterpillar.

"Well, hello, Horatio! It's good to see you again," the Reverend said as they landed.

The Reverend's eyes shone, and a gentle smile covered his face.

"Hello, Reverend. You look great," I said. "Who is your friend?" I motioned to the beautiful red and white butterfly standing next to him.

"Thank you, Horatio," he said. "And may I introduce you to my wife, Katie."

"Hello, Katie. It's nice to meet you."

"Hello, Horatio," she said. "So how do you like being a butterfly?"

"I'm not sure," I said. "Though I do love to fly."

The Reverend turned and asked, "Horatio, don't you even know what you have become?"

I shrugged my shoulders. "Sammy said that we are butterflies."

"Well, that is true," the Reverend said smiling. "We are butterflies, but we are much more than that. We capture the colors of the sun in our wings and carry them with us wherever we go. We bring hope to animals who don't have any, and we send a message of joy to all who see us. We are beauty itself."

I smiled at what the Reverend had said. Then we heard voices from high above. I recognized them immediately; it was Clarence and George. I couldn't believe how much younger and stronger they looked. They were flying very fast, straight down towards The Mud Puddle.

"PULL UP! PULL UP!" Clarence yelled. "You're coming in too fast."

"There is no such thing as too fast," George screamed and pulled up from his dive just in time to put his feet down and skid across the water.

A Dream Come True

"YEEE HAAAWW!!" Clarence yelled as he followed George into the water.

I stood there shocked as both butterflies came sliding towards us. When they reached the bank of The Mud Puddle, they skidded sideways and stopped, spraying us all with water.

"WOW, that was great!" Sammy yelled. He was so excited he could hardly contain himself.

The Reverend, on the other hand, wasn't happy at all, as muddy water dripped from his nose.

He wiped the water off his face and said, "I think you two need to be a little more careful." Then he took Katie's hand, and they walked away.

George turned to Clarence and started laughing. "Ha-ha, I win."

"No you didn't, you cheated," Clarence fumed.

"What do you mean I cheated?"

The two Adventurers argued back and forth until Sammy interrupted them.

"Hey, guys, look who I found," Sammy said, pointing towards me.

Clarence and George stopped arguing.

"Well hello, C.J.," George said. "We heard you turned out to be quite an Adventurer."

"Yeah," Clarence said. "We heard you gave E. Phil Snake quite a run for his money!"

"If you can fly well enough, C.J.," George said,

"Clarence and I have discovered a new adventure. We would like you and Sammy to join us."

"Yeah, C.J., we go Cloud Climbing," Clarence added.

An adventure sounded fun, but I hadn't found Cat yet, and I was anxious to look for her.

"What's Cloud Climbing?" I asked, wondering how safe it was.

"Yeah, what's Cloud Climbing?" Sammy asked, jumping up and down.

"We fly up as high as we can go," Clarence explained. "And when we reach the clouds, we fly right into the center of them. It's really beautiful up there. You should try it!"

George interrupted. "Flying through the clouds makes climbing Ponder Rock seem boring. But don't get me wrong, C.J., Cloud Climbing isn't for everyone. The air inside of a cloud is thick and water collects on your wings, which makes flying almost impossible. You feel as though you will be dragged right back to the ground. It takes a real Adventurer to Cloud Climb."

I thought back to when I climbed the stump on Lightning Limb. I thought about the heavy water on my fur, and how it almost caused me to lose my grip and fall. I had failed then! I had used Traveling Thread. And that is something a true Adventurer wasn't supposed to do. My friends didn't know it, but I was not a true Adventurer. My heart pounded at the thought of Cloud Climbing and having heavy water on my wings. I wouldn't have Traveling Thread to save me this time. There was no way I could go Cloud Climbing, I thought.

"So what do you think, guys? You want to give it a try?" George asked. "Clarence and I are going right now."

Sammy yelled, "Yeah, we'll do it! C'mon, C.J., let's go!"

I didn't want my friends to be ashamed of me, so I made up an excuse. "Maybe tomorrow," I said. "I'm too tired right now. My flying muscles are still new."

George sighed. "Okay, we'll see you tomorrow. C'mon, Clarence, we've got some Cloud Climbing to do."

The two of them jumped off the ground and flew high into the air. Before long, they looked like two little dots in the sky. I felt sad as I watched them disappear into the clouds.

"I'm sorry, Sammy," I said. "I know you wanted to go Cloud Climbing. But I really want to find Cat."

"Don't worry about it, C.J. I understand," Sammy said. "I'll make you a deal. If you'll climb Ponder Rock with me one last time, I will help you find Cat."

"I don't know, Sammy. Maybe I should just wait

around here in case she shows up." Other butterflies had arrived at the Mud Puddle, but still no sign of Cat.

"Ah, come on, C.J. It will only take a second."

"It takes longer than that to climb Ponder Rock, Sammy."

"Not anymore," he said, flapping his wings and lifting into the air. "C'mon, I'll show you."

"But what about the Mud Puddle meeting?" I asked.

"It's just a time for us butterflies to gather around and talk. It's usually pretty boring, though Sandy likes to make new friends."

Sandy had already found a dainty yellow butterfly to chat with.

"Sandy," Sammy called, "C.J. and I will be back soon."

"Okay." Sandy winked at C.J. and turned back to her new friend. "You two have fun."

I just sighed and followed after Sammy towards Ponder Rock. I was still new at flying, but I was not about to let Sammy beat me to the top without a fight. I flew as fast as I could, and I caught up with him at the base of Ponder Rock. We pulled up at HELLO and reached GOOD-BYE before I even knew it. The Rock looked like a blur beneath us as we flew right past THE POINT OF NO RETURN. We made a sharp turn at THE LIFE WATCH, followed by a near miss at HANGING ON.

As we rounded the curve at LETTING GO, Sammy hung back a little, and I could see a huge smile on his face. He stopped flying and hovered in midair. Before I could stop, I had flown past him up to A DREAM COME TRUE, and suddenly found myself surrounded by a cloud of beautiful colors. I had seen these colors before, but I couldn't remember where. A female face emerged from the cloud of colored lights. She was so beautiful that I knew at once who this must be.

"Are you Mother Nature?" I asked in amazement.

She smiled and said, "No, but you may worship me if you like."

Her voice made my heart skip a beat. It was the most beautiful voice in the world. It was a voice I knew well. It was Cat. I looked closer and saw that the colored lights were the sun's rays shining through her multicolored wings. Cat! Suddenly, all of my pain seemed worthwhile. My heart pounded as I realized that what I had struggled to reach for so long was right in front of me. I hovered closer to her and tried to tell her how much I loved her, but I was so excited I couldn't speak. She was the most beautiful creature I had ever seen. But the most beautiful thing about her was the tears of love that slowly rolled down her face.

ᴊp and gently wiped one off her cheek.
ᴌed and said, "I've missed you, Jones! I've
ᴌng for you for so long that it's hard for me
ᴠe that you are actually here."

ᴌ am here, Cat!" I said. "And I will never let anything separate us again!"

We were flying face to face, hovering in the air, our wings almost touching.

"This is called Mirror Flying, Jones. I have never done it before, but the other butterflies tell me it is wonderful . . . they are right!"

I stared into her eyes, trying to convince myself that this wasn't a dream or another memory. Cat was real! I was living in the moment with her. It was a moment that stretched out to include all the wonders of the past and all the perfect possibilities of the future. I reached out and took her into my arms. As I did, my right wing brushed up against hers, and we began spinning. The more we spun, the closer we became. It was like falling in love with her all over again. When our bodies finally touched, our wings joined, and we flew as one. Mirror Flying with Cat was more exciting than anything I had ever done before.

"Cat, you look wonderful, and your wings are the most beautiful things I have ever seen."

Cat smiled at me. "Isn't it amazing how beautiful tears can be, Jones?"

A Dream Come True

I felt warm in my heart, and light and joy where so much sadness had been before. And I realized then how important it is to cry. Crying had let sadness run out of me to make room for good feelings like the one I felt now with Cat.

We flew together for the rest of the day, enjoying the beauties of the meadow and beyond. But as the sun began to set, we knew where we wanted to be: on top of Lover's Landing. I led the way and landed first. Then Cat flew in to make her landing, and a shower of colors danced all around me as before. I remembered, suddenly, where I had seen the colors before. It was in a dream I had long ago right here on Lover's Landing.

"You were with me," I said to Cat. "You were in my dream."

Cat laughed and said, "That was no dream, Jones. I was flying over you."

"You mean, I wasn't alone?"

Cat shook her head gently, "No, Jones, you were never alone. I watched every sunset with you from right up there." She pointed to the sky, which now glowed with the colors of the sunset.

I realized how foolish my fear had been. I had been afraid of being alone, but all the time Cat had actually been right there with me.

We watched the rest of the sunset from Lover's Landing. When the last ray of sunlight disappeared over the horizon, we kissed and then Cat took me to our new home in a clump of wildflowers near The Mud Puddle. It had been the most exhilarating day of my life so far, and I fell instantly asleep in Cat's arms.

Cat woke me up early the next morning. It was dark out, and all the other butterflies were still asleep.

"Wake up, Jones," she said. "Someone wants to meet you at Ponder Rock."

I asked who it was, but she just kissed me and said, "Hurry up, Jones, you're going to be late."

When I arrived at Ponder Rock, no one was there. So I sat down to wait. It was still dark, and I was very tired. In a matter of seconds, I drifted off to sleep. When I woke up, the sun was rising over Ponder Rock. It was going to be a beautiful day.

But, suddenly, the sun began to dim, and as the sky grew dark, the wind became loud. At first I thought a storm was coming, but then a thunderous HOOT echoed through the meadow, and I knew that this was no storm. The sky grew darker and darker, and I felt the clouds wrap around me. Then the wind stopped howling, and the sun went completely black. A beam of light from the sky broke through the darkness and shone down on me like a spotlight. I heard the Owl's voice coming from the light.

"Why have you called me here?"

A Dream Come

I stood there, not knowing what

"Uh . . . because . . . I . . . uh .
minute!" I yelled. "It was *you* who call

"Oh, yeah, I forgot," said The Owl.

The Owl unfolded his wings, and th   ...ght disappeared as light poured in all around me. The Owl had been covering me with his feathers, and the spotlight had been the sun shining through a space at the top of his wings. The Owl laughed as the confusion left my face.

"Now it all makes sense," I said. "My Owl dream wasn't a dream at all, was it?"

"Nope," The Owl said.

"So you were really there?"

"Yep," he said smiling.

"So, why did you call me here?" I asked.

"Because I wanted to tell you how proud I am of you," The Owl said.

"You are? Why would you be proud of me?"

The Owl answered in his big, deep voice. "Because I know how hard it was for you. You were tired, and you wanted to quit, but you didn't. When things were at their worst, you reached down inside of yourself and found strength you didn't even know you had. You hung in there and faced your greatest fear. That makes you something very special."

"What does it make me?" I asked.

The Owl looked at me very seriously and said, "It makes you an Adventurer."

"How do you know about being an Adventurer?" I asked, surprised.

"I know everything that goes on in this meadow," The Owl said confidently.

"Then you should know I'm not an Adventurer," I said and dropped my head. "I used Traveling Thread to climb up—"

"Listen, butterfly," The Owl interrupted. "Being an Adventurer is not about whether you use Traveling Thread or not. It's about living life to the fullest and leaving your mark on the world."

"But I didn't leave my mark on the world," I said.

"Don't be so sure," he said smiling. "Come here, I want to show you something."

The Owl leapt up into the air, and I quickly followed. I thought we might fly off into the meadow, but we didn't. We floated downward and hovered above the ground. As the early morning sky filled with light, The Owl pointed toward the bottom of Ponder Rock at the stone Sammy and I called HELLO. For the first time, I realized it was The Boulder of Doom—the same stone that Sammy and I had rolled down Adventurer Hill so very long ago. The Owl explained that this stone had made it possible for younger caterpillars to follow in our footsteps. I wasn't sure what he meant,

A Dream Come True

until we flew a little closer and noticed two baby caterpillars standing next to the stone. One was short and fat, and the other was tall and thin. The tall caterpillar pointed to the top of Ponder Rock and said, "Up there is the finish line, Harold. And if we start climbing right now, we can be the first ones to meet the sun this morning."

The other caterpillar had a worried look on his face. He looked up and said, "I don't know, Stevie, it looks kind of scary. Maybe we should wait until we're bigger."

I started to understand what The Owl was trying to tell me. We flew back up to the top of Ponder Rock to wait for the baby caterpillars to finish their race.

"Isn't this exciting?" The Owl said. "I always get such a kick out of watching the baby caterpillars on their first race."

I looked at The Owl in surprise. "How many races have you seen?"

"I've seen them all," The Owl said proudly. "I even watched you and Sammy race."

"You did?"

"Yes, but that Sammy really surprised me. I always fly away just before the caterpillars reach the top, but Sammy climbed the rock so fast, that I couldn't get away in time. I think he might have seen me."

I smiled as I remembered our second race when Sammy did see The Owl.

"I must be slowing down in my old age," The Owl said. He looked over the edge by the curve and said, "Boy, that Stevie is making pretty good time. He will be up here soon. Make sure you fly away before he sees you."

"Aren't you going to stay for the rest of the race?" I asked.

"I can't," he said. "I've got to get some sleep. Besides, I already know how it is going to turn out."

The Owl winked at me and flew away. I sat there in silence for awhile thinking about everything The Owl had said, especially about me being an Adventurer. I would be so happy if it were true. Soon, I heard Stevie's voice from below.

"C'mon, Harold, one quick flip, and it's a race to the finish."

I flew up and hovered above Ponder Rock until I saw the young caterpillar pull himself up over the finish line. He stood there staring at the sun.

"Wow, this is even more beautiful than I imagined!" he said. "This is so much better than Adventurer Hill."

Stevie sat down and pulled something from a belt of Traveling Thread around his waist. It was an old brown leaf. When Stevie unrolled it, I couldn't believe my eyes. It was a perfectly drawn map of Ponder Rock. I flew in a little closer as Stevie began to read the words at the bottom of the map:

A Dream Come True

*In honor of Samson J. Caterpillar, who left
his mark on the world by teaching me how to
face my fears and believe in myself. He is my
best friend and the bravest Adventurer I have
ever known. Thank you Sammy!*

Your friend,
Horatio Jones Caterpillar

I felt a lump in my throat as I stared at the familiar
map. Soon, the chubby little caterpillar dragged
himself over the finish line, gasping for breath.

"Oh . . . oh . . . oh, thank The Owl it's over!" he
said, panting.

Stevie looked at his friend Harold and said,
"Harold, this map is great! We're lucky we found it.
With this, we can climb Ponder Rock every morning."

Harold's head began to spin. His eyes rolled back
in his head, and he fell flat on his back. THUD! He
was out cold! Stevie jumped to his feet and ran to
him. He reached down and pried Harold's eyelids
open.

"Harold, did you faint? Adventurers aren't supposed
to faint. Do you think that the caterpillar that made
this map ever fainted?" Stevie looked back at the map
and said, "No, Harold . . . Horatio Jones Caterpillar
was a true Adventurer!"

A tear rolled down my cheek. My heart was filled with pride, and my wings were filled with power. A long time ago, a young caterpillar told me that being an Adventurer was the greatest thing you could be. Now, another young caterpillar was telling me that I *was* one. I said goodbye to Ponder Rock and began flying back toward The Mud Puddle. The Owl was right. I was now the Adventurer that I had always dreamed of becoming. I had faced my greatest fear and accomplished everything that I had set out to do. Sammy's friendship had given me the strength to hold on, but Cat's love had given me the courage to let go. For the first time in my life, I truly believed in myself, and I was no longer afraid. I was an Adventurer, and it was time for me to start acting like one. My heart raced with excitement as I quickly made my way home that morning. After all, Sammy and I had some Cloud Climbing to do!